Chain-Link Fences

Stephen Meiner

Published by Stephen Meiner, 2023.

CHAIN-LINK FENCES

First edition. February 11, 2023.

ISBN: 979-8215122068

Written by Stephen Meiner.

Chain-link fences are very secure and durable fences ...having a very sturdy interconnected weave of heavy steel wire, forming spaces of a diamond-shaped pattern. Unlike a privacy fence or a wall, we can see through a chain-link fence ...and it just seems a bit more friendly to me. Often people are seen leaning on the chain-link fence, talking to a neighbor.

Jesus said we are to love the Lord our God with all our heart & with all our soul & with all our mind ...& we're to love our neighbor as we love ourself. I think it is better to have chain-link fences than walls. You may ask, "Why have any fences?" Well, I do believe part of loving my neighbor is for me to take responsibility ...and that en*tails* not allowing my dog's tail to go into my neighbor's yard to do something that I rightfully believe I should be cleaning up.

The Bible tells us a bit about boundaries, and also how things get cleaned up. Interconnected & woven together with its many supporting verses ...it also gives us an understanding of who God is.

I look at the Bible as truly the 'Word of God'. And hopefully no one puts up a wall to prevent themselves from looking at this.

I will give 5 short 'chapters' of points I'd like to make which I feel are important. I realize my points may not be as important to you ...and likewise not as interesting either. So, to avoid burdening or boring you, beginning with chapter 6, and the bulk of this book, will be short stories.

So, first my serious points ...then a look at my sense of humor, if that's what it can be called.

Though humor is certainly *not* the story's aim in Chapter XVII.

I.—-'Wondering Whose Words'

Wondering whose words (www) ...followed by my 'com'ments.

Or www.com ...referring to the 'world wide web', with someone else's comments. I do admit the internet and my computer are very helpful, and I will resource it when I am making my comments here.

When we do look up things on the internet, hopefully we are aware of who said the things we are reading. And there are always multiple sites we can 'click' on ...based on what we are searching for. We also decide what news sources we follow, whether it is national or local, and we decide whether we trust TV, the radio, printed articles ...or Facebook or Twitter; the latter two perhaps more experiencing the emotion of those venting, though sometimes they may be more 'right on' than other sources. Yet, we do see censorship ...and you and I may disagree concerning what is healthy and necessary.

Yes, we are 'thinking' human beings, and we can be influenced by others ...though we do make determinations as to our eventual beliefs. And I'd think we all have to believe in something. Saying you don't believe in anything, and also adding that you don't trust anyone ...that is still a determination.

I am soon going to 'google' some information, and though I often have little trust that all of the information on the various sites contain accurate information ...I trust that the information that I am about to look up is accurate. I'm looking up Bible verses ...and though some translations may word some things quite differently,

I am not starting out with interpretation, but only the accuracy of quoting correctly what I will use in this chapter ...in let's say the 'English Standard Version', the 'New International Version', and the 'King James Version'. And the part I am looking at is not even the actual quote, as much as *who* it is quoting. I believe many of the other versions, besides the three I mentioned, will also say the same thing.

Let's go to the Gospel of Matthew ...where I believe most versions will all agree as to 'whose words' those are. We could say those are Matthew's written words, but I am asking who Matthew is quoting in Chapter 18, verse 21. Looking at over two dozen written versions, they all have Peter speaking. And those same versions all have Jesus speaking in the very next verse.

Okay, those were easy ...how about the first verse in the Bible. Not everyone believes Moses wrote that, but I believe that he did. Since Moses wasn't around *'in the beginning'*, where then does that information that he put down come from? Well, I also believe that the Bible is the 'Word of God', so if Moses wasn't around when those events were happening, then I sort of believe those words were given to Moses ...by God, so they are God's Words. I've tried my hand at writing books, and it certainly keeps a person busy ...yet one ought to choose a time when there are *not* countless distractions; but I figure 40 years wandering in that wilderness would be adequate time for even someone as slow with writing as me. And if there is doubt about those writings, perhaps reading the Gospel of John, Chapter 5, verses 46 & 47 will help.

I'll go back to an easier one again, but let's keep in mind what was said in the previous paragraph. In Genesis 20:2 ...I believe Moses wrote that verse, but let's look at who Moses wrote as having said, "She is my sister." The over two dozen versions all say that Abraham said that. Then in Genesis 20, verses 3 & 6-7 ...all of the versions say that God is speaking in those verses. And in Genesis 26:7, let's look at who Moses wrote as saying, "She is my sister." Yes, again all of the versions agree, saying Isaac said that. (And yes, *like father, like son* does come to mind.)

In Genesis 11, there is a genealogy listed ...so, who do we believe gave that genealogy which Moses wrote down? My thoughts go back to the belief that I am reading the 'Word of God', and that God is giving Moses the words to write. And furthermore, in Genesis 11:29-30, both Iscah and Sarai are clearly not mentioned as the same person. I don't go outside the Bible for my source of beliefs, so when I see them listed separately, I don't include references which say that Iscah and Sarai are perhaps the same person. To say that, I'd have to lower my view of the Bible and I won't do that. I believe in the authority of the Bible.

Then in the very next verse, I see another verse (which I consider of the same nature as the first couple Chapters of Genesis, where God is exclusively speaking up until Chapter 2, verse 23). Yes, in Genesis 11:31, over two dozen versions present it as the 'Word of God', telling us accurately ...by God telling us. Only the Contemporary English Version refers to her merely as Sarai ...and all the others say she is Terah's 'daughter-in-law'. This may seem to conflict with a reading of Genesis 20:12, where again all of the over two dozen versions say that Abraham, when confronted by Abimelech, tells him that Sarah is his sister—-being as she is the daughter of his dad, but not the daughter of his mom. But that is clearly what Abraham said, not what God said ...as when God is giving us the 'Word', we are told that she is Terah's 'daughter-in-law'.

There is no circumstance where I would refer to my daughter as my daughter-in-law. So, in choosing whether I'm going to believe what Abraham said, or to believe the 'Word of God' ...I clearly am going to believe the 'Word of God'. Yes, the 'Word of God' accurately tells us what Abraham says, just like it accurately tells us that Isaac also says the same thing of Rebekah. And the Bible also tells us that Jacob pretended to be Esau to trick Isaac.

Yes, all the versions I read were fairly in agreement as to who said what ...we just attach a much different understanding of what those verses mean. I think I made a clear point here, yet I hear over and over that Abraham married his sister ...and I don't see that God says that.

Often when I hear that Abraham married his sister, it's after a conversation of how things were acceptable back then ...and the conversation opens to 'the beginning' with Adam & Eve, and incest being the only way to follow God's call for them to 'increase in number and fill the earth'. And I continue to hear the same thing over and over again, of how the gene pool was pure, and incest wasn't *a thing'* to be concerned with because no physical harm would come from incest. Then soon someone mentions, "Well, Abraham married his sister ..."

There are numerous reasons besides the ones I've already mentioned ...as to why I don't believe this to be so. And I consider the subject of 'incest' as very grievous. What is interesting though

...is how readily Abimelech and others accepted the explanation, as the rulers often saw themselves as divine and embraced incest as a way to preserve their bloodline. Yet, I will move on ...

II.—-'People outside the garden?'

The next statement that often ties in with the subject, only makes the knot tighter ...as we try to secure our beliefs.

What statement is that??

To give a little background, most of us are familiar with the account of Adam & Eve ...and how they ate the fruit they were instructed not to eat. And the serpent presented his case to Eve, claiming God was not forthright with her, keeping the truth from her ...having an ulterior motive. Soon afterwards Adam & Eve each gave their versions of excuses why they went against what God had asked of them.

Now, to the statement—-the statement I'm referring to is often leveled against those who attempt to defend the Bible—-yet, it is my preference to not get defensive, but rather to more closely examine what the Bible says, as it speaks for itself.

That ridiculous 'gotcha' statement is: Since Adam & Eve were the only two people, God is responsible for (and to be blamed for) incest ...as there would be no alternative to *fill* the earth, but through incest.

I don't embrace the answers that I hear from those attempting to explain that. Typically, a person hears an explanation, thinks it is a good one, then lodges that response in their head as a ready answer to those who are quick to challenge them on the issue ...in this case, 'incest'. And they say the gene pool was pure back then, so it was not dangerous. I beg to differ ...and having worked in a mental health facility, I am all too aware of how the danger is not just limited to physical harmful effects. You can 'google' it yourself, and read of the immediate mental health damage, not to mention the long lasting repercussions. And then there is also the spiritual aspect.

Yet, even beyond that extensive conversation, I don't see the Bible clearly saying what many people say it says ...and I don't have to change the interpretation or blame the translators to make my point. You absolutely don't have to agree with me ...as I am not asserting myself here above other scholars. I don't have any title, and it even seems strange referring to myself as a scholar ...but nonetheless, I am going to present my case.

It's like in a hockey game where one team scores two goals, and the other team scores five goals. Reading the Bible is not supposed to be a competitive thing, and there is not supposed to be any winning ...but, I do feel good when we can look at these things. And when I read the Bible, I don't think two goals stand up to five, so I look more closely at what it says.

Seriously, I only have one goal ...and that is to draw closer to God, not closer to Him than you, but closer than I am when I am falling away. And I am not sinless, so I do fall away. But, I also feel He shows me things through His Word ...and I do *not* take credit for that, I call it the leading of the Holy Spirit. Yet, that does create some problems ...so, I am careful not to say the Holy Spirit led me to this or that conclusion, as the Holy Spirit is not divisive and I know you and I may not agree.

So, the way I like to proceed, is to allow the Holy Spirit to direct us both in an understanding of the Bible, not creating new revelation to replace the Bible nor having our insights hold more authority than it. I personally believe the Holy Spirit can lead us in different ways ...but, the Holy Spirit does not go against what the Bible says. And it is problematic when Bibles are written to merely paraphrase, and attach a meaning of what we think it should be ...with radically different verses tailored to today's desires, not God's.

The first Chapter of Genesis says, in verse 27: "So God created mankind in *His* own image, in the image of God *He* created them; male and female *He* created them." And verse 29: "Then God said, "I give you every seed-bearing plant on the face of the whole earth and every tree that has fruit with seed in it. They will be yours for food." Ending with verse 31, "God saw all that *He* had made, and it was very good. And there was evening, and there was morning—the sixth day."

The second Chapter of Genesis says, in verses 8 & 15, that the man whom God had formed was *'put'* in the Garden of Eden. It says that God is responsible for the garden being there, and that He also *'put'* the man there. So, it stands to reason that God didn't create the man in the garden, but put him there. Then in verse 16, God quickly tells the man that he is restricted from eating a certain fruit ...a restriction that is not mentioned in Chapter 1.

In Chapter 3, both Adam & Eve eat the fruit they were told not to, and because the serpent had been very instrumental in that decision, this is what the serpent is told: "And I will put enmity between you and the woman, and between your offspring and hers ...", beginning in verse 15. Considering that Adam & Eve had clear knowledge that they would die if they ate the fruit, it would seem like a rather fatalistic feeling of death and depression would be dominating here. Certainly I would not view this as a message of hope. But, in verse 20, there seems to be a shift in perspective by stating that Eve would become the *'mother of all living'* ...not the mother of death, having failed to refrain from eating the fruit.

Why the shift in attitude?? God is an 'encourager'. In Chapter 4, Cain is struggling and God talks to Cain: "Why are you angry, and why has your face fallen? If you do well, will you not be accepted? And if you do not do well, sin is crouching at the door. Its desire is contrary to you, but you must rule over it." Then even when Cain failed in the worst way, he still approached God: "My punishment is greater than I can bear. Behold, you have driven me today away from the ground, and from your face I shall be hidden. I shall be a fugitive and a wanderer on the earth, and whoever finds me will kill me." Then the Lord said to him, "Not so! If anyone kills Cain, vengeance shall be taken on him sevenfold." And the Lord put a mark on Cain, lest any who found him should attack him.

Now comes the decision ...as to whether we will change the interpretation of what we've been told, or stick to what we've been told by holding fast to it, even when it does not seem to make sense along with other verses. I'd rather re-evaluate how I looked at something, and look for more understanding with interpretation, than to ignore all other verses that seemingly would have to have even more wild interpretations to support the one or two verses I am not willing to negotiate. And no, I don't think the Bible is negotiable ...it is our misunderstanding of it which often leads to disagreement.

Now, Adam & Eve didn't do anything nearly as severe as what Cain did, yet sin is sin ...and God deals with sin in our lives. God also looks at our repentance ...and with Adam & Eve, it seems God gave them direction and encouragement. And I find it 'not' hard to believe that God would have explained what He meant when He mentioned to them in the Garden about her seed and the serpent's seed. The pathway away from life was the serpent's way, but Eve was told she would be the 'mother of all living'. All believers today who follow Jesus are on the pathway of the Way, the Truth, and the Life ...of the living.

I do believe that God 'created' in six literal 24-hour days, precisely as it is written ...yet, I also believe that the angels were created before that, and I believe they had some sort of habitat that they lived in. In Noah's time, the earth was destroyed by a Flood ...and the appearance of things after the Flood would be in no way recognizable. And we are told in the Book of Revelation ...that this earth will pass away, and not because of 'Climate Change' (though the climate will definitely change). Yet, a New Jerusalem will come down as our eternal habitation. So, though I don't know what the habitation of the angels looked like, I can clearly see that God acted to cease all coup attempts by quelling the rebellion ...and He started over with the six days of Creation.

And no compromise here ...no, I certainly don't believe man and woman 'evolved'. That's in the category of 'wild interpretations'. I believe men and women were created, 'in *His* image', on the sixth day, along with a man who was *formed'*, glimpsing his surroundings before being *put'* in the Garden ...and during the latter part of the day, a woman was *formed'* in the Garden from a part of the man.

And I believe the eating of the fruit was more of a breach by the serpent. Very clearly, Adam & Eve *did* disobey. But the serpent, invested in his twisted speech, was going against God in a much maligned way. It is one thing to sin, but to deny the sin or criticize the One who holds the standard for right living ...well, that's another thing. While I was growing up, I did not always obey my dad (for whatever reasons), but I always loved my dad and never bad-mouthed him to my friends. I held Dad & Mom in high regard.

But, as I was about to say, I believe there were many men and women created on the sixth day, with only one couple reserved for living in the Garden ...with a taste of paradise. And just like Abraham sent a trusted servant to find a wife for Isaac—-from a land quite far away, being *'his people'* of like-mind—-likely Adam & Eve wanted their children to have spouses who would glorify God, and look to Him for guidance. Cain was sent away, and no way do I see a sister of his being sent away with him. Today, when a crime is committed, only the criminals are sent away to jail or prison, not innocent family. And another point—-Cain being afraid of imaginary people is too much of a stretch for me—-since the claim is that there were only him and his family.

Another verse posited to support only Adam and Eve being created on the sixth day, comes from a statement from the apostle Paul, First Corinthians 15:45, stating Adam was the first man ...yet usually the second part is left out, stating that Jesus is the last man. The genealogy from Adam & Eve—-Matthew's genealogy being that of Joseph, and Luke's genealogy being that of Mary—-are significant as to the 'seed'.

Back to Genesis, "And I will put enmity between you and the woman, and between your offspring and hers; He will crush your head, and you will strike His heel."

So, taking that verse in Genesis ...along with what Paul relates to us in 1st Corinthians, we can see the significance of the 'first man' and the *last man*. Many good men followed God, yet none are relevant to this point ...as at *last* a *man* came as our Savior, named *Jesus*. And many loyal disciples followed Him, yet judgment upon the serpent came through Jesus. Why is the genealogy so important, and what's the significance of the line between Adam and Jesus?? It's important because God is true to what He says. Many children of God were not in the 'physical line', and no 'offspring' holds true for today. If we accept Jesus, we are adopted as His children. And there is no 'demon or serpent seed', as some have claimed. Seeds planted in our minds try to get us to reject Him, but each of us is precious to God and He wants all of us to overcome the enemy.

There is much speculation over what *isn't* mentioned through the first eleven Chapters of the Book of Genesis. And many answers have been given to suffice our seemingly endless need to know what we don't actually know. I'm not suggesting that we shut down our imaginations ...yet, we should not claim a popular interpretation is correct when it is not necessarily right. That is not to say that we should consider the possibility of the Bible not being accurate. I do believe the Bible is true. It seems inconceivable to me that a loving God would fail to preserve that which tells us of His love ...His Word.

In the first Book of the Bible, we are given a view of paradise ...which Adam & Eve could not remain in. But they had been given a glimpse and a hope of a future place. And that same Tree of Life which was in the Garden of Eden will be in the place described in the last Book of the Bible. The Book of Revelation, Chapter 22, speaks of this future abode. And there is healing mentioned, not of individuals, but of nations. In traveling to Heaven, we won't need luggage, but unknowingly we may be carrying a bit of baggage (within us). I don't know ...that is just speculation.

I place a high value on my relationship with God—-and He loves us tremendously. If we don't acknowledge that love, how can it not be void within us—-yet, those of us who *do* accept His love can show evidence in the Bible of Him qualifying each of us as a *'child of God'*. And that ties in with my next point.

III.—-'sons of God'

Sons (daughters) of God ...well, I believe there are two groups of 'sons of God'. The first group would be those angels who did not rebel. And the second group is we 'humans' who qualify under this verse: John 1:12 -—"But as many as received Him, to them gave He power to become the sons of God, even those that believe in His Name."

There is also one reference in the Book of Job 38:7, "When the morning stars sang together, and all the sons of God shouted for joy ..." I don't see the angels shouting for joy at their own creation ...so, does it refer to our creation? And I doubt the fallen angels shouted for joy. The sons of God would be the obedient angels ...as I see it.

As for Genesis 6:2, "That the sons of God saw the daughters of men that they were fair; and they took them wives of all which they chose." Obedient angels wouldn't do this ...and it's hard to believe the disobedient ones (who I don't view as sons of God) would have God's permission.

With those references to 'sons of God', I've found that most people disagree with me as to which group it's referring to in the beginning of Genesis Chapter 6.

My opinion is that believers (or 'sons of God') fell into sin and became involved with those who were not believers ...putting God at a nearly no account status, unwisely choosing to favor worldly standards based upon appearances and desires. Jesus told His disciples that it would be like in the time of Noah ...when 'End Times' would come. And I don't think people married angels back in the time of Noah, and neither do I believe nearing 'End Times' that people will be marrying angels.

One event that I believe angels were involved in ...well, that would be the angelic rebellion. And I believe that event took place before the six days of Creation, our 'beginning'. Placing the rebellion anywhere else would seem to me like 'ignoring the elephant in the room'. When else could it have happened? A huge event of that magnitude would surely be mentioned within the Bible text if it happened sometime after day #1 of Creation. And furthermore, if the angels were created within the 6 days of Creation, certainly they would be as important to mention as grass, birds, or fish.

I personally believe the mention of 'void' and 'darkness' in the 2nd verse of the Bible refers to the existing conditions, as they were, after God quelled the rebellion. Often a thunderstorm can disrupt the electricity in our homes, and the lights go off. Hopefully we have a flashlight handy. With the thunder booming outside, we don't need to be reminded that we are in a storm.

With a different type of storm, it seems most of us need more regular reminders. When driving to work in a snowstorm, a car would be in the ditch and traffic would slow down for perhaps a mile or two, then it would resume to its previous speed until another car would serve off the road. And this interval would happen over and over again, with traffic only briefly slowing down.

When God created the interval for morning and evening, it was precisely how long He felt was needed ...dark and rather void, perhaps as a reminder. Then on day #4, God gave the job to the sun and the rotation of the earth to regulate our needs. And on day #5, God gave us something else that existed with the celebration of Creation ...singing.

Of course, I mentioned that the 'sons of God' celebrated the victory (over the rebellion) and the new plan ...our Creation. Yet, we often don't fully appreciate the continual reminder of that celebration ...as the birds sing, announcing the dawn of each new day.

IV.—-'True, or who copied who?'

My sister was the 'only' girl in a family of six children. Since I have four brothers, I don't know how it felt, or perhaps still feels. I know she wasn't lacking in the department of scholastic achievements. She learned how to read and write at a young age. I'm not sure what age she was, perhaps 4 years old, when she penned one of her first great literary works. On the wall to the basement she wrote that my brother and I were 'pigs'. We couldn't really challenge her assertion nor match her wit, so that stayed on the wall for years (it might still be there). We didn't have Twitter back then, so she was really ahead of her time.

Nearly sixty-five years later, I am able to finally recover from that scathing revelation and am able to write about the event. I don't know if my sister ever admitted to writing it, or she's moved on from petty things ...and joking aside, she is very intelligent. She reads more than anyone in the family, and can even come close to beating us boys in 'Trivial Pursuit—-Sports Edition'. Besides giving due recognition to my very capable sister, the point I want to make is that my writing about the event today, does not place the event within this year of 2023. My name was up on the Marquee ...on that board, making my debut as a 'pig', even before Arnold Ziffel was grunting his way to fame on the TV show 'Green Acres'.

Yes, I came first ...even though it has taken nearly 65 years to acknowledge it. And the event I'm talking about was not for some TV show ...it actually happened. Now, I'm not dis'grunt'led about it, my point is that Moses didn't write about a Flood story because the story was popular. And though it has been said that the Epic of Gilgamesh was written before the account Moses wrote about ...that does not mean Moses claimed part of the story for himself. The Epic of Gilgamesh was written about the time the Bible says the Tower of Babel event took place. And most all the people of that day were close relatives to Noah and his family. The Bible has Noah even being alive at the time. With the Tower of Babel there was much confusion, but they were writing about an actual event ...just being a bit confused about the details, and entertaining certain thoughts of their own. So, whether I wait 65 years to write about something,—-or a thousand years or so later, if Moses then writes about events—-it is not that Moses was an eyewitness ...God was. And it is God who is telling Moses what to write.

We've heard of the 'Holy of Holies' and the 'Ark of the Covenant' ...hopefully, even before the *Indiana Jones* movies. And we saw that *Indy* got slapped by his dad for blaspheming the Name of Jesus. History tells of an entire faith group that was prohibiting the pronunciation of God's Name. And the Hebrew people of the Old Testament even used only consonants when writing it down. It was strictly impressed upon the scribes to also copy Old Testament writings with utmost diligence. And they hid copies ...one of which was later recovered and read by Ezra to the entire nation.

Yet, though the scribes and Pharisees had excellent text, Jesus rebuked them because they seemed to be valuing their coveted positions among themselves more than rightly representing God. Apostles and disciples of Jesus were also highly committed to spreading the Gospel after His crucifixion, and again took extreme care to preserve the writings—-yet it was not long before inclinations began to once again affect leadership in the form of established exclusiveness, this time including Jesus—-but elevating their authority, often claiming equal status to His Word.

V.—-'Is Separation Necessary?'

I believe God chose the correct people who would go to great lengths to give an accurate report about the most important events that ever happened, or will happen. I was told that to *glorify* God ...is to give 'correct estimate' of who He is. I always liked that ...then I thought, we are not merely given an 'estimate'. God makes it very clear who He is ...in His Word, the Bible.

How important is this??

Well, two facts bring significance to this very important issue:

#1) God would that none would perish ...2nd Peter 3:9 "The *Lord* is not slack concerning *His* promise, as some count slackness, but is longsuffering toward us, not willing that any should perish but that all should come to repentance."

#2) Heaven will not be like earth. In other words, there will have to be 'separation' to achieve this.

The 1st statement may be easy to accept, but what does my 2nd point imply? I made a very obvious statement, "Heaven will not be like earth." Perhaps I should add a 3rd point, focusing on the fact that we are all created with 'freedom of choice' ...and are offered eternal life with Him (something a third of the angels forfeited).

Well,—-God doesn't want any of us to be denied being with Him, but there has to be separation from those who choose not to be with Him. And God wants that choice to be a clear choice ...not a confusing one, based upon an incorrect representation of who He is. If we accept Him, God's loving desire is for us to accept Him for who He is; and if we reject Him, God's righteousness would have it that we reject Him for who He is. And the death of Jesus dealt with both those things. Through His *love*, Jesus brought our sins to His crucifixion—-and by accepting Him we are not judged by our sins. Through His death, the *righteousness* of God brings a much different outcome for those of us whose sins define a residence within us ...and are still 'owned' by our refusal to accept His love. And only God knows how firm that refusal is.

That may seem a little harsh, so imagine we are at death's door ...no, that may have more dramatic imagery, but it's after that. Suppose we die and stand before God, saying, "I never had anything to do with You, I never liked anyone on earth who had anything to do with You, and I don't want to spend eternity with You." And suppose God laughs, and says we never knew what was 'good' for us, but He *does* know what's best, so He is going to take us to Heaven anyway ...and we will like it there. Looking at it that way, would we consider it a loving decision, or a total disregard for our feelings? (And we are dragged into Heaven, kicking and screaming.)

Imagine another person dies, and stands before God. Suppose God tells this person, "I never liked you, I never liked the way you hung around other half-committed Christians, and though I know you are more committed than your friends and accept Me for who I am—-well, I am God, and though you've always waited for the day you'd meet Me and join Me for eternity—-well, you made your choice, but I'm not going to honor it. And you're not coming to Heaven." (And the person is dragged away in total anguish, with silent tears amid the shock of betrayal. Yet, I must add that this does not at all depict God's attitude toward us. God loves us. And you're believing a big lie if you think God would ever do anything like this to His people ...to you, or to even seemingly sometimes half-committed me. Yes, we flawed believers join as His family.)

We cannot forget, God knows *'what'* we've been through, *'why'* we've made the choices we've made, *'where'* our heart is, and He knows what befits us ...based upon all that knowledge. We should try our best to lovingly help intervene in people's lives and in decisions concerning our society when we feel our caring can make a difference, showing them a better way. And even when we may think it will never help, we should try anyway ...because we never know. But, we should know that desiring a life without God is certainly not better, and hopefully we can communicate that to them also.

I recall a particular instance, while I was working with teenagers within the mental health facility. The administrators decided that there should be an incentive—-not as great as we have in looking to Heaven—-but, a separation of sorts. They had a new addition built, and weren't quite sure what to do with it ...but, it was much nicer than the old section. So, they decided that the best behaved teenagers would earn to go there ...an incentive, and a reward for their good behavior.

Anytime you group relatively well-behaved teenagers and some 'trouble-maker' ones together, it seldom ever creates a desirable environment. So, this common idea of rewarding good behavior by giving them a nicer living space seemed like a good idea. But, anytime you put a diverse group of psychologists together, it also gets a bit interesting. And in this case it was a bit shocking to me. They decided that for the girls unit, they would put the worst behaved girl on the new unit ...reasoning that she was only a behavior problem because that was what was expected of her, and she couldn't step out of that unfair stigma. (It could have worked, but it didn't. Within a few short days, she trashed the new unit.)

A young man met a co-worker of mine at the mall. He said he had just gotten out of jail ...and he said it was our fault. My friend asked why it was our fault. The young man said he had come to the mental health facility, and that at the time, he felt he didn't have that many problems—-but, he said we gave the impression that it was okay to act out like some of the disruptive teenagers in the group—-and he found it also rather enjoyable, since we didn't do much about it. (This was also during the time when the psychologists felt it was better to not confront certain behaviors. Now, I am in no way bashing psychologists—-there are many good ones, and it's not really about *good* either—-it's about perspective and ideology, and often there are different viewpoints throughout all of society, and the world.)

Speaking of the world, why do we send out missionaries? Some very vocal opinions have been expressed as to whether we should just leave other people alone. My opinion is that sin, left to itself, has a tendency to get worse. And it may get much like it was during the time of Noah. "That the sons of God saw the daughters of men that they were fair; and they took them wives of all which they chose.

And the Lord said, 'My spirit shall not always strive with man, for that he also is flesh' ..."

Again, it says His spirit won't always strive with 'man' ...and the text continues, "And God saw that the wickedness of man was great in the earth, and that every imagination of the thoughts of his heart was only evil continually." And I say that it is of no comfort to me to think we should just let them go down a dangerous path. During the 'Covid' pandemic we sent out vaccinations to help build immunity ...otherwise it was imagined that it could wipe out entire populations. And likewise I don't think people are immune to sin ...and entire populations can suffer great harm if no pathway out of sin is known. I find no comfort in the statement, "Well, as long as it doesn't affect me—-just let them live the way they want to!"

With freedom of choice, we all make mistakes ...but continual calculated maliciousness isn't common to all. There's a saying that refers to 'crossing the Rubicon'. It usually refers to passing a point of no return. Some authors say Julius Caesar reached the Rubicon River at which point he announced *"the die is cast"*, referring to the realization that his commitment was then at an 'all or nothing' point, and he was committed to putting his 'all' into it. The angels who had committed to the outright rebellion must have reached that point also. Obviously they didn't know what the outcome would be (and neither did Julius Caesar, achieving what he set out to do in ruling as a 'dictator' here on earth, though likely not a 'big man on campus' in the afterlife).

Lucifer did not become ruler ...though when thrown down to earth, he has sadly had much success ruling the minds of individuals. And some of those individuals have become those who thrive on leading, and also ruling. And should we trust them with our *'life, liberty, and pursuit of happiness'*? But part of the problem lies within our understanding of all this—-that 'majority opinion' is not often the best measure of what is right, and happiness is not always the best either when it may be at the expense of others.

Personally, I am not merely content with just having my own happiness ...knowing that there are others who are in constant torment and pain. I would hope there is a future time when those people can find relief ...and there actually is a time, and a place. I would be (and am) rather helpless and incapable of making the world better. I don't think I would be wise enough ...I am only wise enough to know I couldn't do it. (And yes, I know I can make the world a better place by doing my small part ...yet, I also know there are people across the world who are not going to directly benefit from my small part. Though I do pray for them ...praying to the One who can benefit them.)

When I said there is actually a time and place ...that place is heaven, but of course, I don't know the time.

Our inheritance in heaven is our promise, though wanting Jesus to return is not something that we should hope would be hastened, as clearly God has not chosen that time to be as of yet. We must all have loved ones who we know have not yet embraced the truth of the love of God ...of which is spoken of in First Peter 1:3-5, *"Blessed be the God and Father of our Lord Jesus Christ! According to His great mercy, He has caused us to be born again to a living hope through the resurrection of Jesus Christ from the dead, to an inheritance that is imperishable, undefiled, and unfading, kept in heaven for you, who by God's power are being guarded through faith for the salvation ready to be revealed in the last time."*

Matthew 6:33 reads, *"But seek first the kingdom of God and His righteousness, and all these things shall be added unto you."*

When Jesus was asked when the kingdom of God would come, we find His answer in Luke 17: 20-21, *"The kingdom of God does not come with observation; nor will they say, 'See here!' or 'See there!' For indeed, the kingdom of God is within you."*

We should all ask ourselves, "What is within me?"

"Can I change??"

Yes, each and every one of us can change.

All at once??

No.

Yet, we can be open to change ...open to His Word, and open to discussing it with others.

Does everyone want to embrace the changes Jesus encourages us to make? Well, we can struggle with that decision ...and some of us don't struggle long, while others take a lifetime to decide.

Like I said, I worked in a prison ...and prisons exist because society deems it necessary to separate certain individuals who seem to have an inclination to inflict misery onto the lives of others.

Before that, like I had also mentioned, I worked with teens in a mental health facility. I know this chapter is becoming long, but it's the area I had worked in for years, and sort of my experience. I will not go much longer, and then onto my (hopefully) more entertaining short stories.

One evening a few restless teenagers were finding some rather bad camaraderie with a few of their peers by finding enjoyment with terrorizing a more passive and peaceful group who were watching TV. I think that anyone who has read this far, or feels they can adequately present their solutions for a peaceful society ...well, they would likely say they side with the peaceful group and are not in favor of the 'bullies' in most any situation. And that was my stance.

I aimed to separate those who I felt were the trouble-makers ...or the trouble-joiners. I sat in the doorway of a room where I had placed four chairs, one in each corner. I directed the first boy, who I felt was the ringleader ...to one of the chairs in the corner. Soon a co-worker sent me another boy for me to supervise ...and in no time, I had four boys, one in each corner. I also noticed that outside the room it had become significantly quieter ...and I assumed, more peaceful. The boy whom I first brought into the 'time-out' room with me got up from his chair and began pacing around, stating that the four of them could overpower me. I calmly said I doubted that. He proceeded to tell me he didn't like my rules, and he preferred 'anarchy'. I decided to pretend I didn't know what that was ...and he enthusiastically told me it was when everyone did what they wanted to do, and no rules. I told him if we had anarchy ...that it would be the same as it was at that moment. He said, "No way!" I told him that I was doing what I wanted to do, and what he was doing was interfering with what I wanted ....and I was going to get my way because I was bigger than he was.

I am glad that God is bigger than all of us ...but, God gives us freedom of choice, so He may *not* do like I did and direct to a separate room those of us who are doing something He doesn't like.

While the one boy was pacing and challenging me, I let the other three boys go, one by one. Then that one boy said he was in the room longer than they were, so why did I let them go first? And I told him because the others were quiet and sitting in their chairs as I'd asked them to do. Immediately, he went to sit down and was quiet ...and I didn't want to lose the point, so I didn't have him sit long. He saw that I was committed to the rules and I had a purpose, and there was some benefit for him in following the rules. And it seems curious on how this boy who initially said he was looking for anarchy, after all, was just looking for fairness. It just took someone to calmly point that out to him.

There is great benefit in following someone who not only cares about you, but also loves you. If you want fairness, it is a very sad story for those who believe God is not fair ...and telling others of their bold stance. If they convince themselves of this or allow someone else to persuade them into believing God is not fair, then how can they desire to be with Him for eternity? And if they don't want to be with God, then I can't even imagine what they think a place without God would be like.

2 Thessalonians Chapter 2—-the apostle Paul says:

"Now concerning the coming of our Lord Jesus Christ and our being gathered together to Him, we ask you, brothers, not to be quickly shaken in mind or alarmed, either by a spirit or a spoken word, or a letter seeming to be from us, to the effect that the day of the Lord has come. Let no one deceive you in any way. For that day will not come unless the rebellion comes first, and the man of lawlessness is revealed, the son of destruction ..."

And Paul continues, "Do you not remember that when I was still with you I told you these things? And you know what is restraining him now so that he may be revealed in his time. For the mystery of lawlessness is already at work. Only he who now restrains will do so until he is out of the way ..."

Yes, it was my small job to restrain some small group of troubled teenage boys. But, the 'Restrainer' whom Paul is talking about is a tremendous influence in 'holding back'—-not just a few wayward teens—-but a vast majority of people who'd turned away from God, influenced by pure 'adult'erated evil (which is not pure at all, as it would be difficult to imagine something being polluted and pure at the same time—-though evil can be so evil that it feels any good will contaminate it).

Okay, am I *adult enough* to admit that I really don't know what the apostle Paul meant by all that?

We are all 'adults', or aspire to soon become so ...and we can all view the record of how people throughout time have viewed God. The only thing that makes sense to me is the 'Word of God', as can be read in the Bible. Let it not be defiled in your mind ...let it be the unadulterated truth.

There seems to be an increasing number of people in 'so-called' advanced society who try to say the Bible has been corrupted and is just manufactured truth. I know of the many translations out there ...and as time goes on, many more are written and seem more interested in being current than being accurate. And with some of them ...it seems they feel a need to be 'up with the times', not understanding that the Bible doesn't need an adjustment, as it is always relevant.

One could say there are slight differences even in the earlier Bibles which we claim were carefully translated. Yet, I contend that all of the written Word taken in its entirety can be discerned. The understanding of His Word does follow much with our sincere desire to understand Him.

If the entire Bible is at first overwhelming for you to even think about, I'd suggest you start with the Gospels—-Matthew, Mark, Luke, and John.

Everything made sense when I read about Jesus.

For me it made sense ...and I believe it can make sense, yes, for you too.

VI.—-'To err is human ...'

Okay, I don't want to lose a point by adding so many points that it's difficult to focus. So now, it's time for a few of my short-stories.

'The Princess & the Poppy' can be found in the series, 'The Evolution of Confusion ...3 of 5 (Train Up a Child ...) & part II, at the end of 5 of 5 (We Should Know ...).

This story happened much before the two aforementioned stories. Actually, this King Lee is the dad, and obviously his son, Prince Lee, later also becomes King Lee ...who befriends King Aling. You will not find them in this story, nor at *Ancestry.com*'.

To err is human ...though likely we'd prefer not to err when faced with an opportunity to 'heir'.

It was a time of Kings ...and kingdoms. They did not mark time, as most only thought of the present, and aspired to the very near future. Sadly, nobody lived very long.

King Lee ruled the largest of all known kingdoms.

King & Queen Lee's first child was a girl. From the time she began walking ...she quickly began to get into everything. What she really liked to get into ...was clothing. She loved 'dress up'.

And she loved looking at herself in the mirror ...then one day she grew out of it. Literally, she grew *up* ...and she had to step back, to get the full version of herself in the mirror. She was only 12 years old, but she felt she was mature. She was no longer interested in dress up ...aside from the royal addition of bracelets, necklaces, rings, and her expensive tiara. This interest had been joyfully anticipated ...after all, her birth name was Jewel.

On this twelfth birthday, King & Queen Lee had promised Jewel her best birthday present ever. They said it may be a few days late, but it was worth the wait. The surprise was ...a baby brother.

It had been no surprise really ...so, Jewel didn't understand why they said it would be a surprise. And Jewel did not see it as the 'best' either. She rather disliked the new addition to the family ...taking so much of the attention away from her.

This birth of the firstborn son ...as it was in every family, brought considerable joy with the announcement of the big event. There was a special blessing, and in rare cases ...an inheritance, though most families were poor and had nothing to pass on. But for the King & Queen, it meant the firstborn would be next to rule the entire kingdom.

And the firstborn son always had two first names, being privileged to have bestowed upon him the first of the two first names ...the name of 'Elder'. The latter of the two first names was whatever the parents of the son wanted it to be. Strangely, some people thought this was simply too confusing, so they then began to refer to the second first name ...as the middle name.

The middle name was actually considered to be of much value, as at times it had become quite problematic in large crowds when people would call out, "Elder!" So, it became the accepted practice to call the older son by his two first names. But with royalty, only the last name was commonly used for the King & Queen ...as it was easier with all the conquering to keep straight which kingdom was the victor.

King & Queen Lee named their son ...Elder Esau Lee. They could not be prouder of their son.

Early on, they felt Elder Esau showed great potential for learning. And at an early age, he also played dress up ...playfully practicing for when he'd become King.

Six years later, Jewel got married to Prince Belee from another kingdom. And that same year that she married, and became Jewel Belee ...King & Queen Lee had a second son. Jewel graciously congratulated them, but she was happy she was not around to hear another crying, hungry mouth.

This second child was named Joseph Jacob Lee. It was highly evident that the King did not take to this child ...and as the years passed, King Lee was convinced that something was wrong with their second child. Queen Lee felt that it was ridiculous to think this of a 4 year old ...but, as more years went by, it was more difficult for her to convince her husband that their second child was normal. Yet, she tried ...and would say that Joseph Jacob was just a slow learner, but he retained well what he did learn.

More years passed, as they do ...and King & Queen Lee decided to visit their daughter. There was much kingdom conquering in those days, and they had not seen their daughter in quite some time. They'd heard of King Belee's death, but thankfully their kingdom hadn't been one of the kingdoms conquered. But, to provide more safety for the new King (also for King & Queen Lee's daughter, now Queen Belee), they'd moved to a part of their kingdom further inland, a recent annex obtained from another kingdom they'd conquered rather easily.

Before their long journey to visit their daughter, King Lee gave the royal scepter to their eldest son, who was now 26 years old. King Lee told Prince Elder Esau that he would be left totally in charge while he was gone. Queen Lee whispered to Joseph Jacob ...for him to behave himself, and stay out of the way of his elder brother. Joseph Jacob was 20 years old ...and had learned some things, mostly to keep out of the way. But, he also learned not to have to be told twice.

But, King & Queen Lee were only gone for a couple days when an uprising quickly developed ...among the women.

Prince Elder Esau advised his dad's royal knights to quell the rebellion by nightfall. But, the rebellion only grew larger.

The rebellion had gotten so much worse, Prince Elder Esau was afraid he'd lose the kingdom. And if that was not tragic enough ...the word was spreading to nearby kingdoms, and the women were mobilizing quickly. They began to call themselves ...the *Women's Movement*.

A young man appears at the castle gate ...insisting that it is urgent for him to talk with Prince Elder Esau. So desperate is he at this time ...that Prince Elder Esau allows the young man to enter his presence within the royal throne room.

The young man doesn't introduce himself, he starts right off talking, *"My older brother, Elder Johnny, is very sick ...and I am merely requesting permission to sell wares at the castle to earn enough money to help prevent my brother from getting any sicker..."*

Prince Elder Esau interrupts, *"The last person who had nerve enough to ask to sell at the castle, sold my family a cow. Hey, I remember, they had a son named Elder Johnny ...you are the Cash family, aren't you?"*

The young man smiles shyly, *"Well, yes ...you do remember. But, honestly, we didn't know the cow was sick when we sold it to you..."*

Prince Elder Esau challenges him, *"It's not just one sick cow that disturbs me ...now that it's coming back to me, your family had a real racket going on. Besides cows, you also sold pigs, swigs, and wigs ...and Elder Johnny had a very silver tongue."*

The young man defends himself, *"We never sold any sick pigs, and the swigs you are referring to were medicinal elixirs."*

Prince Elder Esau seems to enjoy his cross-examination of this young man, *"And what about the wigs ...didn't we have an outbreak of lice at that very time?"*

The young man tries a humble approach, *"Well, my family understood how traumatic it is for some people when they lose their hair, especially the women, and we felt that not only royalty should be able to afford the luxury of having a full head of hair."*

Prince Elder Esau scoffs, *"So, your mom stood up on the back of your wagon ...and beat on two wigs with a big stick, to show the people that your wigs were just as durable as the more expensive ones."*

The young man smiles, *"Yours seems to be enduring quite well ..."*

Prince Elder Esau is no longer amused, *"I've had enough of this, what does selling wares have to do with saving my kingdom?"*

The young man smiles, *"You won't know what I have to offer to save your kingdom, until you first agree to allow me to sell wares."*

Prince Elder Esau angrily interrupts, *"That's insane ... I'm not going to allow the sale of those elixirs. If they are so medicinal, then give it to your sick cows. And I'm certainly not going to have someone standing outside my kingdom, beating on wigs, putting on that affordable hair act. I've heard enough for one day ...for a lifetime. You can leave before I wig out, and have your head for this ...or at least your hair."*

The young man does not turn to leave, *"Your kingdom is about to fall, and I don't believe you can afford to send me away. You haven't even heard my plan yet."*

Prince Elder Esau realizes that the young man is right ...he *is* desperate, and needs whatever help he can get, *"Okay, be quick about it, and tell me your plan."*

The young man happily explains, *"It's my brother, Elder Johnny, who has the wares ...but he's too sick to sell them. They are very useful wares ...you can eat off them. They are vinyl platters with grooves ...so the food doesn't slip off so easy. Johnny is very proud of them. But, for you, he may even make some platinum or gold ones."*

Prince Elder Esau is getting very impatient, *"I wasn't asking about your plan for selling wares ...but, for saving the kingdom! I was asking for your plan to save the kingdom!"*

The young man smiles again, *"No, remember, I said you have to first agree to give me permission to sell my brother's wares. Imagine your Dad & Mom returning to see the kingdom is in shambles, and no longer theirs. And they will hear that it is all because you stubbornly refused to listen to the only one who had knowledge on how to save the kingdom. And you have to start being a little more polite to me also ...or I'm going to just leave, and sell the wares to all those who conquer you."*

Prince Elder Esau grits his teeth, then sighs, *"Okay, you can sell the wares here. There seems to have been a lot of slippage off our ungrooved platters lately anyway ...and it seems that the only ones happy in my kingdom the past couple days are the seagulls, and all those other scavenger birds. They pick up after our droppage, then leave their own."*

The young man extends his hand for a handshake, *"That's more like it ...it's a deal then."*

Prince Elder Esau still has his doubts, but politely asks, *"You never gave your name. I don't recall the Cash family having a second son ...what is your name?"*

The young Cash lowers his head a bit, *"It is not a very proud moment to have to divulge the fact of how poor my parents are. After they registered my brother as Elder Johnny, they could not afford to register me with a middle name. My name is very simply ...Kohlz."*

Prince Elder Esau nods, *"Okay, I will call you ...Kohlz."*

Kohlz doesn't hesitate, *"And I will tell you how to quell the women's rebellion."*

Prince Elder Esau is very eager to hear, *"I'm listening."*

Kohlz explains, *"Well, my selling the wares will help ...because the women like to buy things. Besides selling my brother's platters ...another idea came to me. Women like to play dress up when they are young, but then feel it is no longer mature as they get older, even though they still want to do it. So, I plan to come out with a variety of clothes to sell."*

Prince Elder Esau nods, *"Yes, I agree, that sounds reasonable ...but, why couldn't the women have just come out and simply said what they wanted or what was bothering them?"*

Kohlz laughs, *"You have a lot to learn about the average woman, outside your royal ring. Almost all women will agree that they should never have to tell the men what they want ...they expect the men to know. And if something is bothering them, we men had better know why."*

Prince Elder Esau sighs, *"Well now, I haven't figured it out ...but, that's why you came to me, because you have figured it out!"*

Kohlz takes a quick breath, *"The entire rebellion began with a simple misunderstanding, on one hand ...and my idea of selling clothing should adequately take care of the other problem. But, it isn't simple, I guess, unless you understand, so I'll explain. All you have to do is apologize to the one ...whom you had your knights confront. She was innocent ...yet, an innocent mistake on your part also. I'm sure she will forgive you ...since she is a relative of yours."*

Prince Elder Esau interrupts, *"I know you are doing your best to explain, but I think I'm getting more confused."*

Kohlz tries again, *"I guess I should explain how the problem began ...how it begins, or could with all women. It is often difficult to keep women straight, as they seldom use their last name. Of course it doesn't make much sense to us men, but women don't want to get attached to their last name, because then they'd get too fond of it ...and it just changes when they get married, so they prefer not to use it. So, it's harder to distinguish them ...and when you heard that it was Esther who started the rebellion, you mistakenly thought it was your relative, Esther Kin. But, actually, it was another Esther ...someone well-known in our kingdom to be very impulsive. You just have to know how to handle her ...and I'm speaking of Esther Jin."*

Prince Elder Esau asks, *"How do I handle her?"*

Kohlz smiles, *"Simple ...just distract her. Let her play dress up. I've just started my clothing collection, but I think I have enough to take care of her. The best way to stop her from having fits, is to find something to fit her."*

King & Queen Lee are so proud of their son when they return from visiting their daughter. It had been such a long journey, but a happy one.

Prince Elder Esau stands proudly, giving his report, *"Yes, I single-handedly settled the uprising of the 'Women's Movement'. Now they are selling clothing in the courtyards of every local kingdom ...and the women seem happy. Of course, they can't all afford it, but I price the clothes for ten times as much as it is worth, then tell them it is 90% off. They can't help themselves, and buy more that way. And when they still can't afford it ...well, I tell them they can get it on credit. The husband will then incur their wife's debt ...and will have to work our farms to pay off the debt. Meanwhile, as the husbands are so busy working the farms ...their wives have all the more time to shop for clothing and play dress up, putting them more in debt. We will have enough workers to work our farms until the end of time."*

Prince Elder Esau does not verbalize to his parents how he really feels about the farmers ...critical to the working of the soil, he thinks of the farm workers as no better than worms. And he thinks as little of his brother as he does the farm hands.

Joseph Jacob also does not say anything ...though he knows the truth. That is because he was a part of the truth. Unlike his elder brother, Joseph Jacob had spent much time with the common people ...and he had told Kohlz about the misunderstanding with the two Esthers, during the sudden uprising. Joseph Jacob knew his own brother would not listen to him, but he knew Kohlz was one of the smoothest talkers in the kingdom ...and if anyone could convince his brother, Kohlz could. Meanwhile, as Kohlz had talked to Prince Elder Esau, Joseph Jacob had reasoned with the women.

* * * * * * *

(Bloggers Note: Which person do you feel would have been better qualified to rule the kingdom as the next heir to the throne?? Elder Esau?? or Joseph Jacob??)

VII.—-'Castles of Our Youth'

It was a time of kingdoms.

And though everyone was admittedly living in one kingdom or another, rarely did anyone live like a king ...unless you were in the King's family, and then you experienced much royal pleasure. Most everyone else was quite poor.

The royal family didn't have to demand all that attention ...that's just the way it was, and everyone accepted that, except in one kingdom.

There was one kingdom where one other family got way too much attention. Everyone knew them ...how could they not. They were the Loudly family.

Mr. & Mrs. Loudly went to church every Sunday ...and no one came even close to singing as loudly as they sang. They didn't try to be that way, it was just their nature.

And nature was definitely not excluded from the list of those affected. Throughout the week, the aspen leaves would quake from all the loud laughter from this very happy couple. But even happy couples tend to disagree on occasion ...and when that happened, it was earthshaking.

Many people in the kingdom believe they were half-deaf ...or anyone sitting near them feared they'd soon become so.

There was a saying that went about, that 'there is something in a name'. But Mr. and Mrs. Loudly didn't pay heed to anything like that ...they kept living their mostly happy life in a very loud fashion, not worrying or fretting about what others may think.

One day, no one hears Mr. & Mrs. Loudly ...and everything is strangely quiet, in a disturbing, yet nice way.

The kingdom concludes that either something terrible has happened to them, or something terrible is about to happen to everyone else. It's like walking through the forest, and suddenly you realize no birds are singing, no squirrels chattering ...and you expect danger is looming. Everyone is convinced something must be dreadfully wrong.

Mr. & Mrs. Loudly arrive in church that Sunday, appearing to be somewhat okay, but they can't be! They are too quiet.

Something must be wrong! Mr. and Mrs. Loudly are whispering ...and when it comes time to sing, they sing quiet as a lullaby.

The church is packed that Sunday, and for every Sunday for the next several months. Even the King and Queen attend with their 6-month old prince, Solomon. And if the royal family is there, everyone had better take heed ...and the entire countryside of commoners also fill the church.

They all fear something is wrong, and they'd better cover themselves with the graces of God, just in case something bad is happening. And they aren't about to miss church ...considering the great likelihood that something will suddenly befall them.

It is the fifth straight month in church for the Queen, when she suddenly whispers to the King, "I do believe Mrs. Loudly is growing ...growing and glowing."

The King whispers alarmingly, "What! Do you suppose she is going to explode?"

The Queen laughs softly, "No, no ...I didn't mean it in that way! I see she's got this pleasant glow about her ...and she's getting quite large. I think she is going to have a baby!"

The King smiles at his wife, and half-laughs at his own 'big bang' theory, "That would explain her singing. Instead of their usual loud singing, they are singing like ...like a lullaby, to the baby inside her."

The people seated behind the royal family hear the baby theory, and they begin whispering it ...until the entire church is whispering it.

The following Sunday, church attendance falls off to its usual numbers, and the King and Queen are not in attendance either. The next two Sundays, the attendance falls even further.

Then the following Saturday, the kingdom shakes again. They hear a lot of loud laughter, then a loud sigh ...then a lot of loud laughter, and another loud sigh.

Everyone throughout the kingdom can hear it, yet they don't quite know what to make of it.

They want to laugh too ...but they are afraid.

The next day is Sunday, and they pack the church again.

Mr. and Mrs. Loudly are not at church, but their closest neighbor is ...and the announcement of the birth of twins brings about a quiet laugh of relief throughout the congregation ...and a sigh.

The next Sunday, Mr. & Mrs. Loudly are in church with their twins—-one boy and one girl. The boy is named Isaac, meaning laughter. The girl is simply named Sigh.

As the years pass, for a peaceable kingdom, there are not many stories that are ever told, nor remembered. But, this story is one of the favorites, told over and over again.

This story isn't quite done, as there is much more to be told. The story seems to quickly jump to another generation.

As Solomon grows up, it is also one of his favorite stories, having heard it so many times ...and of course, he is in the story.

Isaac isn't the only one who likes to laugh, but his good-spirited sense of humor draws the attention of Solomon, and they become best friends. Solomon invites Isaac to all the royal celebrations and festivities ...and of course, Isaac's sister is invited also.

With each festival or celebration, there are many games and contests. Solomon is well-schooled, and he usually wins the contests involving cleverness. Solomon is also very athletic, so he usually comes in either first or second in most every event. Isaac is neither very clever, nor athletic ...and he usually loses every time.

Isaac's sister feels sorry for her twin brother, and each time he loses, she gives a big 'sigh'.

Solomon is aware that the losing doesn't bother Isaac. Isaac keeps telling his sister, "It doesn't matter, dear sister, I'm just happy to have such a good friend and to be able to share in the kingdom."

Solomon is pleased with Isaac's friendship, but he also realizes what great love Isacc's sister has for her brother, simply wanting him to do well. And recognizing these admirable qualities and great potential within Isaac's sister, there comes a day when Solomon makes known his desire to marry her.

The news spreads from kingdom to kingdom. The whole earth hears of Prince Solomon's announcement of his intent to wed.

When the day finally comes, everyone knows it will be the wedding of all weddings.

And it certainly lives up to its billing.

Having successfully married their daughter off, Mr. & Mrs. Loudly are content to move to the other end of the kingdom. And things become much quieter around the castle after that.

The following year, Princess Sigh gives birth to twin girls. And Prince Solomon gives orders to the royal craftsmen to build a bigger bed, as his wife wants to have ease with nursing the twins.

The joy is mixed with sadness this year, as Solomon's mom, the Queen ...dies.

Two years later, Princess Sigh seems to be taking after her mom, as she is getting huge. She soon has triplets ...adding three sons.

Prince Solomon orders a still larger bed, to incorporate the baby boys.

Though Solomon insists he and his wife need no help taking care of the two 2-year-old girls, and the three baby boys, the King tries to help the best he can. He hasn't been the same since his wife has died, but he tries not to show it.

Solomon is concerned for his dad though. He decides to call on a good friend. Isaac will be more than willing to help his sister. Mr. & Mrs. Loudly would help too, but they had caught a sickness, and do not want to jeopardize the health of the five little ones.

Isaac is a big help. And it gives Solomon's dad a bit of relief ...being able to be with the family during the day, but also affording a good night's sleep. This helps lift the King's spirits somewhat. As the year comes to a close, and the next year begins ...the King is much better.

Then as another year marks itself, Princess Sigh gets really huge. Seeing how large she had gotten with the twins, then how much larger she had gotten with the triplets ...Prince Solomon can't imagine how many babies his wife is going to deliver this time.

But then Prince Solomon has to experience something he can't imagine ...life without his dad.

He will miss his dad terribly ...this goes without saying. It wasn't that long ago that he had to face life without the absolute best Mom in the world, and now losing Dad just adds to the emotional heartache. He is quite aware that he is in no way prepared to be King, yet news travels quickly ...not only about his dad's death, but about the now new King Solomon.

Solomon knows his wife can deliver any day now, and he just can't deal with it all. This time Isaac takes on the responsibility to call upon the craftsmen for a bigger bed. And the craftsmen say the bed will be ready in two days.

Isaac's parents are well now, and he will call upon them for help too. And Isaac tells Solomon they will also be there in two days to help.

Isaac thinks of a clever scheme ...a bit of a short-cut. His parents live across a large lake dividing the kingdom, but the lake is much longer than it is wide. It would take several days to travel around the lake, but Isaac figures he can row across the lake in one day, and then one day back.

Isaac recalls how he and Solomon had competed in events when they were young, and how Solomon always beat him. But, now Isaac is feeling good about himself, and he makes the trip across the lake in one day.

The next day, the three of them get into the rowboat ...and again, it starts out as a peaceful day and he is sure they can make it by nightfall, but then it becomes an entirely different story. Clouds move in, and the wind picks up.

The wind is initially in their favor, and aids his rowing ...but, then the wind really picks up ...the waves becoming larger and larger.

Standing on the balcony, at a high point of the castle wall, Solomon stares out across the treacherous waters. He can see them. It would not be that much farther, but he can also see the worst is yet to come.

King Solomon stands there, praying silently that they will make it. For the past several years he has watched Dad's health fade, seemingly losing his 'will to thrive' after mom died. And now, having lost Dad too ...he faces the reality that he may be losing his best friend at this very moment.

The common folk had traveled from afar after hearing the recent news of their new King. They gather below, awaiting some royal announcement and anticipating some sort of speech along with a formal coronation ...and mostly, perhaps a feast afterwards. But, as they look up, they wonder why he is not speaking. From where they are standing, they cannot see what King Solomon sees.

Solomon looks beyond the crowd, down the road from the shop by the side of the lake, to where the craftsmen are carrying the newly commissioned bed.

Solomon looks back over the treacherous waters ...and sees the rowboat capsize. He can barely see them hanging onto the overturned boat, and they don't seem that far out ...though perhaps still too far out amid those violent waves.

He feels so helpless, watching them clinging desperately onto what will inevitably soon disappear ...and them with it.

Solomon suddenly realizes the craftsmen are nearest that part of the lake, and that they are looking in the direction of the Loudly family. They must see the life-threatening situation before them, why are they not attempting to help?

But, Solomon knows why. They are so loyal to the King, they must deliver the bed ...and they likely fear their King would be displeased if they set out to do anything but that.

King Solomon wants to shout, but he knows the craftsmen will be unable to hear him. If only they were not so wrapped up in serving him, without giving thought to his character as King ...and what his true heart's desire would be.

Solomon tries to scream out to the craftsmen, waving his arms and pointing, "Use the bed ...hurry! Go!! The bed!!"

But, the craftsmen don't hear him ...and they slow down their pace, as they continue to look towards the drowning victims.

The King screams inwardly, "What kind of King do you think I am? No bed is worth more than a human life ...nothing is!"

The commoners begin to disperse, having thought the King was upset with them gathering beneath his balcony, seemingly hollering out for them to hurry, and go ...to bed.

King Solomon suddenly gets an idea. He hollers, "No, *great* people, don't leave ...thank you so much for coming. And we will have a feast soon. Just do this one thing for me."

The commoners stop, and look back up to the King, waiting for his command.

King Solomon hollers, "Everybody together now ...Sail on Queen Sigh's bed ...Sail on Queen Sigh's bed ...Sail on!!"

King Solomon raises his hands ...as if to orchestrate the chorus.

The commoners begin to chant, louder and louder, "Sail on Queen Sigh's bed ...Sail on Queen Sigh's bed ...Sail on!!"

The craftsmen hear, and respond ...and even use the sheets as a sail. And Mr. & Mrs.Loudly, and their son Isaac are saved.

From that day forward, the most popular bed is Queen Sigh's bed ...or as we know it today, a Queen-size bed. (and...especially a bed on sale, or was it a sail on a bed—-or was it the aiding of the bedding for the sail: as was told of—-the great heroics of the craftsmen with their aiding and abedding? ...and though it's spelled 'abetting', it would have been a crime not to save them.)

Now you know to what great lengths I will go to for a joke ...and a couple of bad ones at that. But, I'd been watching Rocky & Bullwinkle with our young children, and along with that humor—-besides, Peabody & Sherman, and Fractured Fairy Tales, well, that was my influence, along with being too tired to make up my own bedtime story. So, I did come up with this, and now you know how I respond under pressure.

And at least it was intended for a good ending, if not for good humor!

Castles of Our Youth ...where, in our minds, we explore. We find adventures and bury treasures deep within our childhood, often forgetting where we put them.

It is good to remember.

VIII.—-'Rats, we had the same idea!'

I remember ...those long days, while I was working in the prison. I'd often have to work a double shift ...so even when I got a day off, it always seemed like I was catching up on my sleep.

My bed was a much coveted place, but our children were very young, and they would say, "Tell us a bedtime story first!"

I often remember saying that I didn't know any bedtime stories, to which they'd say, "Mom just makes them up ...just make one up!"

And I'd usually say, "I'm not good at telling stories like Mom."

It was at this moment that the guilt would impact me in a big way. After all, what greater moment is there for children to make known the cumulative desires of their hearts, those end of day testaments of their love before falling asleep ...those endearing moments with Dad & Mom.

We had taught them all to pray, turning their hearts towards God, as they crawl into bed each night.

What kind of witness would I be, if not to encourage them also to freely desire that quality time with the very ones who had told them about God ...and all about how loving He is.

I was truly amazed, as a story did pop into my head ...and it became their favorite.

It is a story about rats who like eating baked goods of all sorts ...whether it be casseroles, breads, cakes, or pies.

It so happens the Queen loves pies ...and her birthday is coming up very soon.

The King decides to have a huge party for her, inviting the entire kingdom. He says he will provide the main dishes, his only request is for everyone to bring a pie.

When the rats hear of this, they invite themselves.

The pies are all placed in the huge palace banquet hall, and everyone hides throughout the palace, waiting for the King to escort the Queen into the adjacent throne room.

Everyone is poised to holler, "Surprise! Surprise!!"

They holler even louder, repeating a second time, "Surprise! Surprise!!"

But, then the surprise is on them as they enter the huge banquet hall together.

We all know why pies have slits in the top of their crust, but the rats didn't know ...they were just thankful for it. For them it was a quick and easy point of entry. And they had begun to devour the pies from the inside out.

The Queen is handed a silver knife with a diamond studded handle, so she can cut the first pie. And when she does, they all hear a loud squeak followed by several terrifying noises ...one of which is the Queen shrieking, as rats come darting out of pies from all over the hall. The Queen shouts, "Pie-rats! Pie-rats!!"

The guards from the anteroom, upon hearing the screams, think the palace is under attack and begin screaming, "Pirates!! Pirates!! Raise the drawbridge, secure the castle ...and save the King and Queen!!"

The Queen hollers frantically, "No, don't raise the drawbridge ...I want those dirty rats to escape!"

The King begins to laugh, the Queen begins to laugh ...then everyone begins to laugh.

The Queen chortles, "This surely will be the most memorable birthday I've ever had!!"

Of course, with me having to explain what 'chortle' means, we all get to laugh ...as I try to chortle.

(Years later, our children are with me at the library. One of them walks up to me, handing me a book about 'Pie-rats'. Out of curiosity, I looked at the 'copyright' date, and saw the library book was printed even before our children were born.)

The children do believe me that I made up my story. And though someone had thought of the same theme, the children told me that my version was better.

I found it kind of curious how the same idea which I thought was original, worked into the story of a well-known children's author. I had only one book in print, 'The Evolution of Confusion' ...and I had thought I'd like to write a children's book next, but that trip to the library sort of dimmed my hopes on that endeavor.

But, I can enjoy what other people have written ...and we have a good collection of children's books. My favorite of all time is *'Tell Me the Secrets: Treasures for Eternity'* by Max Lucado.

Be ye like little children ...

IX.—-'Attempting to move mountains ...'

In the marketplace there are many interesting smells, sights, and sounds. The once fresh fish, scales glittering in the hot sun, will soon be given to the stray cats, for the pungent smell would soon drive customers away. The delectable aroma of pies and other baked goods seem to get stronger in the heat of the day. But so does the smell of the animals, and that's why they are kept at the other end of the marketplace.

At one stand, the wives gather about the colorful fabrics and sewing materials, while their husbands inspect hides and leather works. In addition, most everyone sells apples or peaches and a variety of beans, peas, corn, tomatoes, and potatoes.

Bleating sheep and mooing cows are paraded before a judge, the best usually sold for breeding. The sights and sounds blend together, with laughing faces enjoying the merriment of games and contests. There are contests for adults, children, and animals. Running frantically through mazes of hay bales, squealing pigs search for the finish line. Young boys and girls cheer as their friends tumble about in sack races. There is much laughter and playful shouting. But there are other sounds that are barely heard, hidden in soft whispers.

Occasionally, a boy or girl will whisper something in the ear of another. It is all done in the name of fun, and is good and acceptable. The teasing actually helps spur on the competitiveness of the games. But there are other whispers that are not good, and they are not done in playful jest. These whispers are known as gossip, and they are often hurtful.

For gossip to take place, it has to involve others. But others have their options also. They often join in the gossip, and help spread it. With this, the whispering can soon become a buzz, and can be as destructive as a buzz saw in reckless hands. Another option is to just ignore it, and not get involved. Nara considers neither of these options. She is moved by compassion, and can see the hurt and the damage gossip can cause. She extends her kindness to those that others are gossiping about. And that usually means they gossip about her also.

****

The best smelling pies at the marketplace obviously draw the biggest crowd. And of course, it always helps business if someone is as friendly and outgoing to everyone as Nara is.

Everyone knows Nara because of her grandfather. Aaron is always the first to be called when someone needs help. For those living in the country, he is the only medical help for miles, being both a doctor and veterinarian.

Nara will never forget that event ten years ago. She was only five years old when the barn caught fire. Dad and Mom had both rushed back into the barn to save more of the animals. They were able to get out of the fire, but collapsed from smoke inhalation. Grandfather said if he'd arrived a few minutes earlier he could have saved their lives. And he still struggles with the 'ifs' of that dreadful day.

Grandfather still does his doctoring, while Nara takes care of the farm. Tanned by the sun, you can tell she loves the outdoors. And when the autumn time of market arrives, she is proud of the work she'd spent pruning trees in their orchard, as they are known to have the best apples around. Having cared for Nara since the age of five, Grandfather now boasts of how she mostly takes care of him. She does all the cooking in their small wooden shack, and her specialty, of course, is pies.

Many of these apple pies are displayed at 'market', as well as secret recipes of wild berry pies. The aroma alone attracts a crowd. Eating appears to be one of the favorite things to do at 'market'.

Nara runs her hand through her strawberry blond hair, then reaches down to pet her lamb. She takes her lamb with her everywhere. You could say they're inseparable. If not for her, the lamb would not even be alive today.

She can't help think animals and humans often behave similarly. Just this year, late spring, this black lamb was born, the runt of the bunch. Nara didn't understand why, but Grandfather had explained to her that animals often reject certain ones of theirs ...solely because of color, or because it's a runt. Grandfather had smiled, happily stating, "I'm very proud to say that you are nothing like that ewe ...and I love you, very much!"

Grandfather was bothered by the fact, and would often repeat himself, "Just because they are different," he would say, "...and sadly, you'll often find people are like that too."

Nara looks up, as she hears the gossip begin to fly, "Here comes that lowly son of Lem and Blanche."

"Figures, for mountain people to name their son, Root."

"Well, the way they talk, how do you know the parents are actually Lem and Blanche; it could be we'd not heard right ...it could be Limb and Branch. Limb, Branch, and Root ...wouldn't that make fine for a family tree!"

The whispers are low, but the laughter is loud.

No longer whispering, one sings aloud, "Nara has a little lamb, its fleece as black as soot; and everywhere that Nara goes, is that 'sootie' lamb and Root."

They laugh even louder.

Nara feels sorry for Root. He seems nice enough; and he and his parents don't make a fuss about not having much. It always seems like those who have the least, also complain the least.

Root catches Nara's sparkling blue eyes, and comes around back. He pets her lamb. And Nara slips him one of her pies. In fact, it is the last one. She knows he wouldn't be able to afford one, and he always seems so grateful.

One of the men sees this, "Nara, how about one of those fine pies of yours?"

Nara looks up, "Sorry, I don't have any left."

The man grumbles, "Yep, that last one just seemed to up and disappear!"

****

Grandfather and Nara get up early. The second day of 'market' is not usually as busy as the first, but it is no less important. Today they will be judging for the best pies.

Nara goes out the door to tend to the animals, but she returns quickly, and Grandfather is pained by the look on her face. "Grandfather, Grandfather ...my lamb is gone!"

The evidence is clear that someone had stolen her lamb. Nara is so upset ...that she cannot bring herself to bake any pies. She will not win the blue ribbon this year. She is more eager to see the sheriff.

The sheriff is always at the market. He not only feels he should be present at a gathering of that size, but he enjoys the excitement. This particular morning, Nara provides most of the excitement, "Sheriff, I'd like to report a stolen lamb."

The sheriff tries to pride himself with a calm demeanor, "Now, Nara, let's not jump ahead of ourselves. How do you know the lamb was stolen? How do you know it didn't just get loose ...and run away?"

Nara's eyes now sparkle with tears, "Because we had left my pet lamb in the pen on our wagon."

The sheriff smiles, clearly using his superior logic, "Well, isn't it possible that your lamb could have somehow escaped from its pen?"

Nara cries, "I'm sorry, I'm so upset ...I forgot to mention that the wagon is gone!"

The sheriff calmly replies, "So you are also reporting a stolen wagon. In that case, I do believe the two are connected, so, yes, I do believe your lamb has been stolen."

****

It is noon, and the sun is much hotter than yesterday. Grandfather is already called upon to help a lady who is suffering from heat stroke, and he suspects he will be called upon several times more before the day is through. Yesterday, he'd had a much easier day, only having treated one man for overeating.

The sheriff returns to Nara, "I think I have a lead. Wasn't Lem and Blanche's son, Root, here yesterday?"

Nara does not understand the purpose of the question, but answers honestly, "Well, yes, he was ...but I don't understand what that has to do ..."

The sheriff interrupts her, "Wasn't he spending a lot of time around your pet lamb?"

Nara's heart begins to pound, "Yes, but you don't really think ..."

The sheriff interrupts again, "Yes, I do really think ...but it's not just my thinking. I have witnesses that say they saw Root early this morning ...and he was not walking. From the rain we had last night, I believe that wagon made some deep tracks. And from the heat of that sun right now, my guess is that those tracks have dried so hard, it will be a cinch to follow them."

****

The sheriff and a few men take to the task, and by late afternoon they have Root in their custody as they return to the market with the stolen wagon and Nara's pet lamb.

As the sheriff asks his deputy to take Root to the jailhouse, the marketplace buzzes with the fresh new gossip, "I knew that boy was no good. You just can't trust a mountain man ...even if he's just a boy. It's the way they are brought up."

"Yeah, with a mountain man around, it's easy to find the Root of the problem."

"I saw the way he was looking at that pet lamb. I'm surprised they didn't find him eating lamb chops. I hear they'll eat dog, if it's not their own."

"I'm surprised he didn't 'up and steal' Nara. You see the way he always looks at her too."

"Yeah, we were easy on him by going to the sheriff. We knew he was guilty of stealing that lamb ...we should have lamb-basted him ourselves."

Grandfather speaks up, to the sheriff, "Before you have your deputy take Root in, I'd like a word with you."

Nara is in tears. She feels relief that she has her pet lamb back ...and sheds tears of joy for that. But those tears are mixed with tears of disappointment. She doesn't understand why Root would do a thing like this. She knows that just because you show kindness to someone, that doesn't mean that person will offer their sincere appreciation. But Nara feels she is a fairly good judge of character, and she was sure Root was genuinely grateful and she could trust him.

The sheriff agrees to assign two men to a particular area of the marketplace. The men do not understand their assignment, they only know they must do what the sheriff orders them to do ...and they know the order came after a request from the doctor, Aaron.

****

The third day at the marketplace, Root stands with Nara, helping her sell some of her pies. She hadn't won the blue ribbon, but she sells more than anyone else because everyone knows they are the best.

At first many people at the marketplace are outraged because Root is not in jail. The rallies of whisperers grow with their claims of injustice upon hearing that the doctor and his granddaughter were not pressing charges. It is still not right, and the mountain man should be locked up. After all, he is a thief ...and he will likely steal again, from someone else.

"If I catch him stealing from me, he'll wish he were protected behind those jail bars."

Then the tide turns, per se. There's much talk out & about the marketplace, but it is of a much different nature. No more hidden whispers. The ones who'd begun the whispering, are now no longer listened to ...they have no one to help spread their gossip. And these guilty ones are now the ones who feel they need to hide.

The talk now is loud and travels far, of the doctor's cure for gossip and prejudice.

****

As the facts became clear, Nara's grandfather had been treating a man for overeating on that first day at the marketplace. He had the man quietly resting, when he heard whispering behind the tent.

Aaron heard what they had planned to do. But instead of going to the sheriff at that moment, he decided it best to let the men carry it out ...and perhaps learn a lesson.

As planned, the men stole the wagon with Nara's lamb. They hid the wagon just before a fork in the road, waiting for Root and his parents to pass down the other road on their way to market.

Two of the men waited further down the road to market, beyond the fork, meeting Root and his parents. They told Root that Nara had gone to his place and wanted his help with something. Root turned around, and could see the wagon, by then a good distance down the road. He shouted for Nara, but it was too far. He began to run after her, as his parents proceeded on to 'market'.

Little did the men know that Nara's grandfather, Aaron, had told his granddaughter the evening before, after they'd returned from their first day at market, that he had some doctoring to do. Aaron had gone to the mountain shack to talk with Root and his parents about what he had overheard earlier that day. So the men who felt they had a foolproof plan, had no idea that their plan had been heard, and they would never have guessed the mountain family would soon be acting in agreement to go along with it.

Before Aaron had left the mountain shack that night, he made a pie and did some doctoring on it. He had arrived back home late that evening, as Nara was used to him doing with his medical rounds. She did not see him place the pie on the buckboard seat of the wagon.

Aaron knew that whoever came to steal the wagon early that morning, would think it was one of Nara's pies. The day before Aaron had also heard one of the men mumbling about wanting one of the pies, but Nara had given the last one to Root. Aaron was sure the pie on the buckboard seat would be too much to resist. No one could resist one of Nara's pies!

Aaron had figured that since Root would be traveling on foot, he needed to allow just enough time ...as the sheriff would be tracking on horseback. The sheriff easily followed the hardened wagon ruts to the mountain shack where Root was caught with the evidence of the stolen wagon and lamb.

The sheriff had promptly arrested Root. Aaron was certain that the sheriff would stop at the marketplace to return the wagon and Nara's lamb, because they'd have to pass by there on their way to the jailhouse. And that is exactly how it happened.

At that moment Aaron had taken the sheriff aside, telling him of what he had heard the day before ...and of the pie he had doctored. The sheriff agreed to post two men outside the outhouses at the far end of the marketplace. Soon it was evident who the guilty parties were. And soon their little party of dishonest fun would be over.

****

Nara is so happy Grandfather's plan had worked: to help flush their system of that contagious gossip.

Sadly, sometimes there is a dishonest pretense involved with a willingness to offer friendly help. But with friends like that, who needs enemas ...obviously, they did—-and sadly, it often involves sitting down and bearing out the facts. In this case, it was painfully effective in extracting the truth.

Prejudice, bias, and hatred are taught—-but sometimes the greatest lesson is in learning we were wrong ...having the courage to admit it ...and asking for forgiveness, as well as forgiving those who have wronged us.

X.—-I don't think my friend would mind me retelling it.

A few years ago, I became friends with a Christian who'd left the University in Baghdad, coming to the United States. He told me a story that is a parable of sorts commonly known where he grew up in Iraq.

The story speaks of how different cultures may approach and choose to deal with what they may perceive as a problem with the elderly.

This particular 'people' told a story of a time when ...

It was generally agreed upon that it was too burdensome to continue to attempt to care for the elderly among them. When it was deemed that one was too old, it was the responsibility of that person's oldest son to carry him on his back. In this fashion the son would carry his dad up the mountain, and throw him off the cliff.

It was not just common for this to take place, it was expected. Yet, it was also expected that during that long trip up the mountain, that neither the dad nor his son express any emotion. Neither would talk at all ...after all, what could be said?

About halfway up the mountain, the dad says, "Son, are you okay?"

The son had not expected his dad to speak, and answers with an unprepared and uncomfortable tone of surprise, "Why do you ask?"

The dad offers a bit of advice, "Perhaps you should rest a bit; you look a little tired."

"No, I'm fine!" answers the son, abruptly.

The dad persists, "No, I'm serious!"

By the tone of his voice, it's obvious that the son is frustrated, "You know that everyone says it's best not to talk. You know this must be done; you're just attempting to prolong this! What must be done, must be done."

The dad insists, "No, I'm not trying to prolong this ...seriously, you don't look well."

The son's tone reflects increased frustration, "I'm fine ...and we're not going to rest. We're going on! And I'd appreciate it if you'd not make this any more difficult than it already is. I will be very thankful if you'd not talk to me anymore!"

There is a long silence. They are three quarters of the way up the mountain, when the old man begins to laugh. He starts out in low, and his laugh builds in intensity.

The son shouts above his dad's laugh, "What is so funny! The laugh is even worse than your talking! If you must, tell me what is so blamed funny!"

The dad chuckles, "I'm sorry, but I think we should stop; I don't think you are in that good of shape. I don't think you can make it."

As nervous sweat pours off his forehead, the son screams, "I've never felt better in my life ...I'm not even sweating!"

The dad laughs, "Oh, I don't know about that ...I don't think my grandson, your son, would see it that way!"

The son, knowing how much his own son truly loves grandpa, cannot handle such a statement as this, "Dad, you know this must be done!"

The dad laughs once more, then gets serious,"I'm sorry, son, you know how much your son enjoys tracking ...how he tracked that wolf that was killing our sheep. I didn't mean to make this so difficult for you. But I honestly don't feel you are in that great of shape. I mentioned that to my grandson. Can you be sure he's not following us? He is a good tracker."

The son looks back, "I don't see him."

The dad laughs, "Neither did the wolf. And what did you tell your son when he asked where you were going this morning?"

The son feels it is hopeless to expect his dad to comply with not talking, "I told him I had to take care of you."

The dad takes a more serious tone, "Just yesterday I told him all about how I took care of you when you were young ...after your mom died. You know how much your son loves his grandpa."

The son is totally exhausted as they reach the top, especially emotionally, "And I suppose you told him all about the trip we were going to take today. Of course, you weren't supposed to, but you haven't done any of this right, have you? And I suppose you told him that making a climb like this takes a heavy toll on a body, and by the time I reach the cliff, I'll probably be an old man myself ...and he'd might better throw me off the cliff too ...and save himself a trip later on."

The dad says, "Well, you can take your chances ...and think what I'm saying is just a bluff, but you'd be taking a big chance with a rather deadly bluff." And the dad looks momentarily at his son, then leans forward to peer down the rocky crag.

Suddenly a young voice chimes in from around the corner, "Grandpa, that looked like fun ...dad is really strong, isn't he? But, I don't think he can carry you back down too ...he looks too tired, and I'm too small to help out."

"You are a wonderful grandson, and you are more help than you realize. If we each give your dad a hand and take it slow, I think your dad will be able to make it back."

Arm in arm ...the three of them, turn around, and start back down the mountain.

XI.—-Ain and Cable

This is a different sort of story.

A country at war.

An eight year old son, Seneca, seeing that his family may be overthrown and likely killed, dresses up as a commoner and hides among a group of children all near his age. As tragedy unfolds, it all happens so quickly ...and furiously. The kingdom is soon overthrown, and most of the families die ...only the poor children remaining.

The children are carried off into captivity.

In a year's time, another King & his army, led by General Guardian, resolve to rescue the children. They overthrow this kingdom which the children have been enslaved to, and aim to restore the previous ravaged kingdoms ...resettling the children in their land.

The young Prince Seneca does not want to rule, so when they are returned to their land ...he hurries to the ruins of his parent's royal residence. Only he knows where the book of *Names & Families* is hidden, and he burns it to destroy the record of him being the prince and rightful heir to the throne. Seneca confesses untruthfully that he is a common thief, and had once stolen some of the royal jewels ...showing a necklace and a ring that was in truth his, but which he said he stole. He spun the story, telling 'Guardian' that while stealing the jewels he had read in the royal book of the name of the heir to the throne.

Seneca is desperate. He knew his commoner friend, Ain, was very possessive ...and would be too eager to become king. Yet, he felt his other friend, Cable, was rather insulated and detached from those around him, and therefore also not very capable to rule others. But, more than anything, Seneca is certain he does not want to rule.

With his king's permission, General Guardian helps them restore their old kingdoms, and believes Seneca when he says he had read the royal book. Seneca says the book had also included dialogue by the royal family, stating that they'd feared one day they may be overthrown, as they were too large a kingdom, and too inefficient. Seneca reveals that it was suggested in the writings that the kingdom be split into two halves, with each of the royal family's two sons eventually ruling an East and West kingdom. And Seneca tells Guardian that the two sons are Ain and Cable.

Now, Ain and Cable knew they were not brothers, but Ain liked the prospect of being a ruler ...and threatened Cable, getting him to agree not to tell.

Guardian says he will assign a couple of his best soldiers to help Ain and Cable until they get older ...and Ain and Cable both like this idea. But, first they secretly and privately thank Seneca ...telling him he will be a welcome guest in any of their kingdoms. They admit they were rather shocked when he had lied to Guardian, but it is their secret, and they will never tell anyone.

As the many years pass, Ain and Cable pass away, and their children's children become princes, then kings. Guardian had also passed away, and his grandson, Draug, is not so kind a ruler. Draug likes war, and particularly likes conquering.

Draug conquers the East and West kingdoms, and decides once again to combine them into one kingdom ...which he decides to rule himself. But, he rules rather inefficiently ...and in a couple years he gets too ambitious, trying to add a third kingdom, and loses it all.

The descendants of Ain and Cable both decide that they are the rightful heirs ...and each claim that they have proof that their descendants had not been brothers. The obvious conclusion is that one family is an impostor. Of course, neither family has any proof, but they feel they don't need it ...as any claims they've stated, they hold as true.

******

Today, we have a similar problem ...we are heirs with Christ Jesus, yet we sometimes profess claims that somehow allow us to feel we have greater standing with our authority of that claim.

Now, I don't know how one can have any greater authority than the words of Jesus, nor how anyone could possibly add further stipulations to the wondrous fact that He has given us the assurance of our salvation. And I am certainly able to rejoice in knowing I am heir to His kingdom in Heaven ...and do not have to be rebuked for thinking I earned it because I did not, and none of us do. I am not entitled to more of a standing (or sitting) with Him in that heavenly abode than anyone else. I only aspire to reside in Heaven, under His loving care.

Also, to be an *heir*, is not to be in *error* over how I can somehow establish my standing here on earth ...as if anything I can do here on earth can be more highly valued than to witness to someone about the simplicity of them also receiving the gift of salvation through Jesus.

I'm reminded of the mom of a couple of the apostles asking if her sons could have that exalted position to sit next to Jesus in Heaven.

I exalt Jesus, and I do not desire any special position ...it is such an overwhelming statement of grace on His part to even allow me to be in Heaven where I can be somewhere in His company. My name is in the Book of Life, and to know that ...is so comforting. Where I sit, stand, or walk is all going to be in pure delight.

And my job here on earth is in testifying to whom Jesus is ...so others can better know Him. To what degree anyone sincerely embraces Him is not known to the human mind ...and it is not in my job description to even guess at it.

We also should attempt to use discretion with what kingdoms on earth we choose to reside in. We should be a friend to those in need, but also befriend those we need to encourage us in the areas we should dwell in. (Philippians 4:8, says we are to *dwell* or think on certain things.)

******

(Our oldest son likes sports, so he said he probably would've chosen to reside in the kingdom with Cable.)

XII.—-'More mountains ...'

The majestic mountain seemed to touch the sky. Its top was never seen, as there was never absent ...some sort of cloud circling the peak.

There were four streams which flowed out of the mountain. The common people who lived in the region never gave much thought to it, though one family was very meticulous about facts and history. The facts had to be passed down, of course, as the frontiersmen who initially came to the mountain were no longer alive. But, the great grandfather of Lester Adams had written it down ...as his dad had told him, and his dad's dad. And there were maps, the oldest of maps showing only one community, the first settlement in the area. Yet, it was clear that the region had been thoroughly explored, as the four streams were also mapped out.

The old map simply labeled the streams: West Stream, North Stream, East Stream, and South Stream. Rather simplistic, but those names held to this present day. The only settlement on the old map was simply named *West*.

There were other maps, the second oldest having a small settlement named *South* ...on South Stream, of course. Later maps included the settlements of *East* and *North*, on those respective streams. Today, all the settlements have grown to somewhat equal size and population ...and are called *West Community*, *North Community*, *East Community*, and *South Community*. The initial families in the settlements had always kept to themselves for the most part ...and there was no real communication between *West, North, East,* or *South*. The reason that the settlements grew so substantially was that suddenly gold was discovered, and though each of the settlements didn't know it ...each of the four streams were equally rich with gold.

Each of the communities grew from many outsiders hearing of the news ...and each of the communities shared their biased feelings about the unfriendliness of the other communities in the mountain region. So, there remained virtually no communication among the mountain communities. They just 'mined' their own gold ...and built churches and courtyards of the precious metal, and as far as word could travel the report was that their extensive worship was unparalleled in any land.

One day while worshiping, Les Adams felt led to reach out to the other communities in the region ...so, he got his family together to voice his intent to visit *South Community*. There were no objections ...so they went.

As they are greeted in *South Community*, Les does the talking, "We want to extend our friendship as an expression of unity."

Mayor Moore considers this a spiritual journey, and greets Les and his family with open arms, giving them the Grand Tour. Mayor Moore tells them that *South Community* was the first settlement in the mountain region. Les and his family are on a journey of peace, so he chooses not to mention all the documents and maps in his own community's possession.

Mayor Moore takes them to the Town Hall, and shows them countless documents about the authenticity of his statements. Les notices that the documents ...well, the papers just seem too, too ungenuine. The documents seem to all be of the same approximate age.

Afterwards they are finally taken to the place of worship. Mayor Moore has a big smile on his face, "I've saved the best for last!"

The place of worship is equally as beautiful as where Les and his family worship, but Mayor Moore is full of surprises ...and his smile grows. He is obviously proud of his community ...and who wouldn't be, as it looks to be a very fine community in every way. After all, though pride is most often looked on as not a good thing, it frequently is really just proper satisfaction ...and encourages people to do good things.

But, then the shock comes.

Mayor Moore speaks with quiet boldness, and rather glibly, "Do you know that the South Stream, flowing into our South Community, is the only stream that actually has real gold? Others have heard from afar of this famous Gold Mountain, with four communities and four streams ...all having gold, but we are the only one that truly has real gold."

Les Adams had experienced how welcoming Mayor Moore was to him and his family, how gentlemanly he was being ...and he'd been polite enough to not say the other communities were only mining Fool's Gold, but that was the implication. Yet, Les does not want to offend, nor dispute the claims. Les merely seeks to return the Mayor's politeness by inviting him to visit West Community.

Others are beginning to gather for worship at this time, and seeing that the mayor hesitates in responding to his invitation, Les thinks that it is perhaps because the mayor doesn't want the others to feel left out by the singular invitation. So, Les extends his request, "We would be glad to have as many of you who would want to visit our community ...you are all invited, and welcome."

Mayor Moore sees the group's hesitation, and as mayor of the community he feels obliged to answer, "I guess we pretty much all feel that our worship here is so satisfying ...that we feel our Lord would not really approve of us worshiping to any less degree than our worship here. But, you are always welcome to join us in our community, and at our church here."

One other gentleman does speak up, "Yes, we feel our Lord has ordained our worship here, having established us as the first settlement. Our life in South Community was clearly established here by our Lord's providence."

Les takes a deep breath of the fresh and satisfying mountain air ...yet, an air of aloofness among this friendly group of people surrounding him is sadly what impresses him most; polluting his hope of that spiritual bond he'd intended to create by this visit.

(I guess, the bottom line is ...each of us must decide for ourselves how we view all of this, Moore or Les.)

XIII.—-'Science class ...'

Philosophy, and science ...do they support each other??

The task for a high school drama class was to put on a play to address the question: How did we come to exist??

So, let's set the stage:

A caveman character, Flint, presents his dilemma to another, "It's so unfair ...look at her!"

Other (Stoney): "Whoa-man, I see what you mean ...she's a real knockout!"

Flint: "Yeh, whoa-man ...that's what she is. Yeh, a real knockout ...you knock her out, hit her with this persuader."

Stoney (pointing): "It's like those two."

Another caveman is resting his club on one shoulder, while dragging his catch by her hair.

Flint: "Yeh, how fair is that? She gets a free ride!"

Stoney: "We need to change all that. We need to grow our hair long."

Flint (pointing): "Yeh, ...look at that guy. He's pretending to be unconscious, while she drags him."

The man being dragged winks at the two of them.

(Scene switches to a man and woman dressed in robes, standing within Greek columns.)

Philosopher (to his wife): "Are you ...'in the family way'?"

Wife: "Yes, I believe I am ...and *you* are just plain in the way. Why don't you go to the Agora, the Lyceum, the Forum ...whatever you call it, just *go*!"

Philosopher (at public forum): "I think, therefore I am."

Fellow philosopher (Socrat): "I am ...having problems with moving this large column that fell down. Could you help me with it?"

Demcrat: "Why don't you ask Pythag ...he may have a theory on how to do it more easily."

Socrat: "I did ask him, but he is still working on some angle on how to get out of doing any hard work. I will never get it done if someone else doesn't help."

Demcrat: "Okay, we will work together to right the column."

After working hard together to 'right' the column, Socrat is exhausted, and sits down against the column. Sweating, he wipes his brow, "Now, where was I ...ah yes, I think, therefore I am."

Demcrat raises his arm to also wipe his brow, but as he does, he turns his head ...getting a whiff of his armpit, "I stink, therefore I am."

(Scene changes to a famous model joining her husband on a polar expedition.)

Kate: "Why didn't you tell me to change clothes?"

Kate is wearing skimpy clothes, while several men stand around in long, thermal underwear.

Polar bear dad: "We almost got killed trying to get a picture of that babe playing on that ice floe ...they always tell you, just go with the flow."

Polar bear mom: "Who are you trying to kid ...everyone knows you can easily swim 200 miles. Truth is, you almost knocked each other out trying to get a look at her."

One of the men wearing long, thermal underwear, "It's near impossible to figure out the dynamics."

Kate: "I don't know what you guys are thinking—-you can talk thermodynamics all you want, just use whatever dynamics you need to get a move on, and get me some of those thermals—-I'm cold!"

Polar bear dad: "Now that ruins my day!"

Polar bear mom: "Now, let's look at this logically ...what does she have that I don't have?"

Polar bear dad: "Logically ...philosophically?? I saw, therefore I am."

Polar bear mom: "Kate's on Facebook ...I'm not on Facebook, therefore I aint."

Polar bear daughter: "I text, therefore I ...ahem."

Polar bear son: "I tweet, therefore I'm lame."

Polar bear mom (to polar bear dad): "I think, therefore ...I conclude our son takes after you. I think he may be bipolar."

Polar bear dad: "Boys will be boys."

Polar bear mom: "At any age, that is. Why do you encourage that stuff?"

Polar bear dad: "Don't worry, SI somehow got ahold of all his photos. And I think Kate likes the penguins better ...she'll likely never return here."

Polar bear mom: "Why do you *Kate-r* to this sort of thing? Can't our son just play video-games like a normal cub?"

Polar bear dad: "Us adults already have a bad ...

Polar bear mom: "Bad enough grammar? It's *We* adults ..."

Polar bear dad: "Wee adults sounds like small—-and, are you kidding, there is nothing small about us—-so, as I was saying, us adults have a bad enough reputation. I don't want to ruin it for the cubs. Yes, it's partly due to our size, but also because of our appetite ...that they think we're too violent. And video-games are too violent, like that 'climate change' one ...it had too much *gore*."

Man with wild hair, driving a DeLorean, drives past the polar bears ...past the cavemen ...then past the Greek architecture and philosophers, as one of them says, "I think, therefore ...what was that?"

The wild-haired professor parks his DeLorean time machine outside a schoolhouse. He walks inside, and enters a classroom of junior high kids, "This is wild ...I know, I know, you're saying that I'm wild. I ask you ...do I exist? Or am I just a 'pigment' of your imagination?"

Student: "You must be real ...my imagination isn't *that* good!"

Professor: "I contend that if you believe in evolution ...then I don't exist. But, sadly to say ...neither would any of you. But, don't tell your parents that some weird substitute teacher at school tried to scare you today. You do exist, and you do have parents ...and whether you like it or not, I am your teacher. Today, I will try to show you how you exist."

Student (same one): "So far, I exist in boredom."

Professor: "We're all bore-dumb, no need to stay dumb. And of course you're bored now, I haven't even begun. If my looks don't excite you, then perhaps the main interest of most kids your age will work ...like, we're talkin' food."

The professor then takes out several bags of marshmallows, all different sizes and colors ...and a couple boxes of toothpicks.

Professor: "This is like the *'marshmallow challenge'* ...but we are going to use just marshmallows and toothpicks, instead of raw spaghetti noodles, tape, and string. And you don't have to just use one marshmallow ...you can use as many as you want. But, we are not building towers ...instead we're going to build molecules. Each marshmallow represents an atom, and you link them together with the toothpicks in any design you want to ...to build molecules. It's kind of a race, and I will tell you when you can start ...but, you will only have 30 seconds. I also baked some marshmallow pies for afterwards, and some of you may want seconds on that too."

Another student: "Do we make as many as possible, or do we try to make one as big as possible."

Professor: "This is supposed to be the evolutionary model, so there are no set rules ...now, on your mark ...set ...go!!"

The group of students do surprisingly well. The professor notices one student who made no molecules, having spent the entire 30 seconds popping marshmallows in his mouth, "I see one of you spent your entire half minute consuming, not creating ...but, that's okay, that would also happen randomly in evolution. What is your name, young sir?"

Student: "My name is Adam."

Professor: "That figures. You did say your name is Adam, not atom, right?"

Student: "Actually, I'm Adam Jr. ...and my mom's name is Evelyn. And I like all kinds of pies, unless I'm now going to be forbidden from having some because I didn't make any molecules."

Professor: "Actually, you made something more important ...you made a point. And this is going to be rather interesting. While you are all eating the pies I brought, I will try to do my best putting forth both arguments ...and you can all decide what makes more sense. Some of you may think I absolutely cannot be fair, as I already said I don't believe in the evolution of humans ...but, I think I can be fair. And if any of you think you can do better, I am more than willing to listen to the case you want to present for how we came to be."

Adam: "And when you begin to make your argument for Creation, do we also get seconds on pie?"

Professor: "That depends how big your first piece is. And yes, my second case will discuss the Creation account that we read about in the Bible ...and about Adam & Evelyn. Sorry, don't tell your parents I talked about them. I mean ...we will talk about Adam & Eve."

Adam: "Don't worry, my parents don't care who talks about them ...especially, Dad. He doesn't usually care what strangers say because they don't know him from Adam."

* * * * * * * *

Half a dozen of these stories directly mention kingdoms. We often think of castles, crowns, and adoring crowds of people gathering about the many walls and fortresses built. Yet, there's often much poverty that exists very near those kingdoms.

Though it's exciting to imagine, visualize, and often to write about ...the kingdom that's important to me is the Kingdom of God. Yes, the world does much to emphasize inequality ...and look at all the poverty, yet what did Jesus mean when He said, "Blessed are the poor in spirit ..." (Matthew 5:3)???

How about today?

A couple years ago, a friend of mine was living in a box. The government took away his box, and gave him a sheet of aluminum foil. They told him it was a solar panel and 'green energy'. He later moved to a new area of the city, and got himself another box. He was happy until they found him ...and he was foiled again.

Kidding aside, we should not put God in a box ...we have a much bigger picture in the Bible, so we certainly don't have to imagine how to perceive Him. We should not come to God with haughtiness and being self-satisfied in our hearts, but humbly realizing we are impoverished and spiritually empty. Should we be indifferent if we have it good, while others are struggling? No, we should be grateful & pray for others. There's no inequality with God ...we can all come to Him. And He does *know us* from Adam.

XIV.—-From Big Bird to 'the birds and the bees' ...

Two parents thought that it was time to educate their two sons on the subject of the 'birds and the bees'. They had considered their sons to be still a bit too young, but the neighbor convinced them that kids now-a-days learn very early on ...and if the parents don't tell them, then the kids will hear about it in a much less desirable way from their peers. The parents had confidence they gave their children a rather good spiritual background by reading them Bible stories, along with other stories at a very young age ...actually, since they were infants. So, they were probably mature enough now, to move on from *Big Bird* to a much bigger *'birds and the bees'.*

Here's the conversation between the two sons, Bill and Phil:

Phil: "Solomon had 700 wives ...I wonder how that worked out?"

Bill: "Yeh, Dad says he has a hard enough time working out 'his' work schedule ...I wonder how Solomon managed his?"

Phil: "I guess Dad had to learn from his own dad ...and seems like I remember hearing that Grandpa used to have a combine."

Bill: "What's a combine?"

Phil: "I don't know too much about it, but Solomon had 300 of them."

Bill: "I'm glad Dad doesn't have any ...but what would Grandpa do with one?"

Phil: "Well, I think a combine did lots of things a wife didn't. That's why she's called a combine. I think Grandpa called his 'Betsy', yes, I think that was her name."

Bill: "What did Betsy do?"

Phil: "I think Grandpa said she did three things."

Bill: "Who needs one ...Mom does more things than that! What did Betsy do that was so great?"

Phil: "Grandpa said she reaped."

Bill: "I don't know what that is, but Dad says you reap what you sow. What else did she do that was so special?"

Phil: "Well, she did something called threshing."

Bill: "Thrashing?"

Phil: "No, that's a temper tantrum. I said 'threshing'. It's sort of like 'loosening' and 'separating'."

Bill: "Solomon would have had to have done alot of 'separating'. Grandpa might have only one, but Grandma is better than a whole bunch of combines ...so who needs 'em. And I think I recall Grandpa saying that the youth today should make sure not to get a 'loose' one, so I don't think I'd even want to take a chance."

Phil: "Me neither. I think the other thing Betsy did ...was winnowing, yes, that was it."

Bill: "What's winnowing?"

Phil: "I'm not sure ...but, I think it involves two things. I think I remember something about blowing lots of air."

Bill: "Is that like when she talks too much?"

Phil: "Probably ...but, I think it also has to do with getting rid of pests."

Bill: "I guess there's always a few of them ...especially if there's 300 of them, I'm sure Solomon had his share."

* * * * * ** * * * * *

As Phil and Bill get older, they become a bit more familiar with what things mean ...and how combines differ from concubines.

Phil is excited and happy. Bill can tell he's onto something by the fact he's humming, and he recognizes the tune from the *Aladdin* movie ...'*A Whole New World*'.

Bill can't contain himself, "What is it this time, Phil?"

"It's not a magic carpet or lamp ...this is better. It'll open our world to a whole new understanding ...of *girls*!"

Bill is not convinced, "Nobody will ever figure them out!"

"But we have something that nobody in Ma & Pa's generation ever had ...it's called the *internet*."

They are at the age where they're interested in dating ...but it's not called 'dating' anymore, it's called 'talking'.

"We aren't even *talking* to any girls yet ...what good is that?"

Not being discouraged, Phil tries *Google*—-*'Looking at girls'*

The top response is: *'Eye contact can be powerful'* ...(yet, it is followed by a *'but'*, as a warning.)

"Let me try ..." Bill tries *Google*—-*'What signs are there for when a girl likes a guy?'*

Again, the response is: *'Eye contact'*

No, too risky ...they both agree. Not ready for that, we've got to be more discreet.

Phil tries *Google*—-*'When a girl likes a guy, what are some things she might unknowingly do?'*

The top response is: *'She plays with her hair.'*

Phil gets excited, "Let's see how that works! But to be safe, let's observe some young people first."

"What young people?"

"Mature young people ...like college students."

"You mean, young adults ...but we aren't adults yet."

"We can pretend to be! We live in East Lansing ...we can just walk right in on one of the campus parties."

It'd be easy to get in, but maybe not to get out ...they agree.

Instead, Phil and Bill opt for tickets to a home football game.

And what makes their real reason for being there easy, is that MSU wins!!

The cheerleaders stand in the background as a sportscaster is interviewing one of the star players.

Phil tries to contain his excitement, "That girl ...look!!"

"Where?"

"Over there!"

"Over where?"

"The cheerleader ...just to the right of the sportscaster."

"Oh, the one flicking her hair?"

"Yes, that's a sign ...that means she likes the guy."

"Wait, look over to the left ...that cheerleader talking to one of the football players!"

"Wow, she's really flicking her hair!! She must really like him!"

"Or maybe the constant flicking means she has head lice."

"Well, maybe *he* really likes her then ...he's not stepping back out of range."

"Lice can't jump, and though she's flicking a whole lot, I think he's safe. Unless she has fleas ...they can jump, yet we can too. Let's just make sure we're not jumping to conclusions." Bill tries to dial back his sarcasm.

"I'm kind of sorry I suggested this. It's not really helping my confidence with girls. I think we should *flee* this mission and go home."

"Yeh, studying girls is too risky. If we get caught and one says 'Get outta my hair!' ...that would certainly make me feel like I'm the *louse*."

XV.—-'Can't see the forest for the trees ...'

Yes, we often can't grasp the big picture ...simply because we are looking at only what comes into our immediate view, or that which is introduced into our minds for the time.

Yet, sometimes we do look at the big picture and still don't understand. It may be during those times that we should take our minds off that which we are not quite yet prepared to deal with ...and attempt to appreciate and be content with what is solidly before us.

Well, enough about forests and trees ...how about the absence of trees, or any vegetation for that matter.

An endless wandering across hot desert sands.

No end in sight ...and worse yet, no water.

Or is there? Could it be?? I want it to be ...but, does my desperate 'wanting' bring me any closer to reality?

Perhaps it is just a mirage ...what I want to see.

But, now I miss what I'd convinced myself that I never would. I do not like the scorching heat, yet a little warmth would be welcome now!! ...as I'm about to freeze. My tongue is cooled ...but, I can't feel my hands or my toes.

And soon I will feel nothing.

Okay, now the snow melts ...but, I didn't know it was so deep. With the 'snow ratio', there'd have to be a hundred feet of snow. Who'd believe I'd soon be drowning?? I wanted water, and a little warmth ...but, I think I'm ready to admit I don't really know what is best for me.

Yes, I've gotten myself into some deep dilemma here!!

I'm raising my hand to acknowledge that ..."I give up!!"

Yes, it is hard to admit, but I need help.

Correction ...I need saving!!

So much for that sequence of thoughts. Maybe the heat got to me. Actually, we *are* in a desert ...we've always been in a desert, stretching for miles and miles in every direction. We don't travel too far ...never have. Why?? Because we've found an oasis. Not a mirage, but a real source of water. Not much water ...but, just enough. A satisfactory amount to survive ...and that is what life is about.

It's hard to imagine a small stream ...not to mention a lake. Yes, a lake must be a fantasy ...the fancy of outlandish minds. They call themselves creative thinkers, but we call it insanity ...howbeit, a pleasant fantasy.

Someone described an ocean once ...more far-reaching than the desert sands. And it has been told there are four or five of these oceans ...all connected to each other, and enough to drown all the desert sands.

No person would claim that sort of insanity ...how can anything be any bigger than the sand and the sky??

I like to watch the bugs ...they fascinate me. Though I know that bugs my parents, especially Mom.

I feel I'm much like the bug. The bug lives in its limited world, and I can see all of its busy activity. I sometimes wonder if ...and who watches me?

Mom doesn't like it when I study the bugs ...especially the ones she calls *flies*. They mostly live in the area we visit a couple times each day ...sometimes more often, depending on how many leaves we eat. Dad says the flies come from what comes out of us, and he says that we probably somehow came from the flies. Mom says we got contaminated by what the flies get their feet in, and that our brains are full of it too. I wanted to ask, "How can we come from something that comes from something that comes from us?" I can't quite follow Dad on that one, nor Mom's remark about our brains. Yet, if Mom makes no sense, no ignoring the fact she makes dinner.

I try to keep quiet, so I can keep full. Not much you can do with just leaves, but Mom does better than either Dad or me. I would never challenge Mom on how she prepares the meals, but I somehow suspect she adds some flies. She made up this strange word, called protein, and says I need some.

Dad says he was there when I was born ...and insists that he is right. But, Mom still insists that isn't true ...that I didn't come from the same place. Mom says Dad does not know squat ...and that was not my 'born' position.

Dad laughs ...saying Mom insists she came from a rib. He said Mom listened to great-great Grandma, whom he says got crazier before she died. What Dad thought was crazy, was that Mom had begun to listen to great-great Grandma. Crazy old Grandma had said she'd been the only *old* person to survive a crash. And she'd said they had all flown into this desert, and the desert sands blew over everything, covering the evidence. Dad said the only evidence was that she was crazy.

I kind of have my own idea ...but, my head hurts when I think too hard. I see it differently, because I have a logical mind. Instead of us coming from flies, it makes sense that flies come from us ...since they appear on the stuff that comes from us. And they must be more advanced ...since I could never dream of flying, nor am I as efficient with my other activities. The flies have so much energy, but on occasion I get tired ...and have to sit down, or squat.

Don't get me wrong ...Mom *does* really love Dad. She just feels he limits himself by what he sees ...yet, sometimes she says that works out better.

By that ...you may think I'm not using my logical mind. Yet, logically, if flies come from us squatting ...and that foul smelling substance comes from us, then flies come from us. We must be the center of life. But, Mom says I came from a womb, technically hers, and not from what Dad says ...excrement.

It's possible that Mom could be right ...as Mom always smiles when she looks at me, and Dad often frowns and wrinkles his nose.

Mom says Dad has a difficult time looking beyond the oasis ...but, that's because he thinks all looking is done through the eyes. Mom says a person doesn't have to see only that which is near to him ...but can see with their mind, or as she says, her heart.

Mom has told Dad before ...that it doesn't mean that she wants to leave the oasis. She is afraid just like he is ...to leave the water, their source of life. But, it doesn't hurt to think beyond oneself.

Mom dreams ...and Dad does not like that. He says it is not practical. How can we believe that there is so much wonder and beauty ...when all we see is sand?

Mom says she dreams of big oceans of water and glorious lush things to eat that grow among leaves.

Dad says all he has ever seen is leaves ...and more leaves. He also says that if there is a glorious Person who gives her dreams of oceans and lush fruit ...then why doesn't this Person give *them* endless waters and plentiful fruit?

Mom often says, "We have to be where we are, before we will be where we will be."

Dad says, "I can no longer stand by and let you fill our son with all those insane thoughts and empty dreams."

Mom: "If we came from a fly, as you say, when did we lose the ability to fly? And if a fly came from us, clearly it is more advanced than we are. Yet, I'd think that any creature that spends much of the day around a dunghill isn't an advanced species by my way of thinking. But, isn't that precisely what our son is doing ...spending his days being fascinated by flies, and staring at dung?"

Dad: "I agree that our son must be taught things ...but, I came up with my ideas first. That should qualify me as the primary teacher."

Mom: "Well, by all means then ...go join our son, since you can claim squatter's rights."

She didn't mean to make him mad ...but, she knew he was. She was not happy when he was not happy. It was just the way it was with her ...the way she felt it was supposed to be. She imagined it was supposed to be the other way around too, but it was not the driving force within her to demand she be made happy. She wants to please him ...and yes, though she often fails, she can't really help that.

And she couldn't help the nightmare she had that night either. The nightmare he probably would have just found funny, but there was also a dreamy part of it. She didn't want to share that part with Dad, but she had to share it with someone ...so, without much thought put into it, she shared it with me.

She saw the ocean again, meeting the sand ...and a creature that she had never seen before. Then she saw an image of herself at the same place ...yet, much nearer and touching the water. She was not pleased with the uncomfortable position she was in, though she did say she attempted to grin and bear it.

I love Mom ...she is so beautiful to me, certainly more beautiful than Dad. This is a wonderful image to me, though somehow I feel I am invading her privacy. It's some sort of weird garb she described to me ...and she is glad I was not in the dream to see this strange pleasurable squatting.

"Son, I don't want you to think I too am into some sort of worship over these things of strange nature and base beginnings. Necessity is not always the mother of invention ...yet, there are times everyone does find it necessary to squat. Just don't draw attention to it!" This is what she told me ...and she is convinced it had some significance.

Mom has her doubts. She apologizes, as she had never intended to share it with me. She resolves never to share it with me again, yet she's eager to share something else with me. After asking me to close my eyes, she asks me to imagine as she describes the pleasant dream she'd had. She recalls the dream where things did not evolve from base beginnings. Things began with splendid wonder. But, there was a sense of lack of appreciation for what was ...and a view that things could be different. Not always a bad thing, unless it is achieved through taking away from some ...usually to merely benefit a selfish desire of another.

Obtaining more should not come about through our expecting others to accept less ...and certainly should not be achieved through deception, nor through force.

In the dream, when this happened, all the splendor disappeared ...or at least it appeared to. It was hard to tell because everything was dark. There was violence ...and then it became dark.

At this point, I didn't even realize that Mom had left ...to allow me to dream on my own, or if not *on my own*, for the dream to take over in my *own* mind.

A sense of who I am ...is in the dream. I am siding with those whom violence was done against. And the violence certainly was countering the splendor ...and I did not want the splendor to be lost, or cease to exist. What madness would it be for a new order to rule the ruin??

Then a vision comes ...and we are no longer in darkness. I sing along with the 'much singing'. Though the darkness does not disappear entirely, it is separated by intervals. And each time the vision returns, it is no longer dark for that interval, and something splendid returns. Not the same, but nonetheless ...splendid. And each time we sing ...we celebrate the gift of each day.

Something else happens too. We not only begin to trust the interval—-knowing that when it becomes dark, that the light will return on schedule—-but, we also begin to trust that there is peace and hope beyond just trusting the cycle. We just know there is a glorious Person behind our salvation from the darkness ...and those who sing testify to that fact.

When I wake up ...I know that dream had great meaning. There is no way I am going to believe that life comes from something as lifeless as hot barren desert sand ...*that* kind of belief cannot be true. Nor can I then ignore and somehow attempt to formulate beliefs counter to what I believe...that a somehow unimaginable non-life can become living. It would be not that much different than staring at that dunghill and expecting great things to happen.

No wonder one can become so despondent. We need to rely a little less on our prideful knowledge, and follow a little more wisdom.

Or humble ourselves, not to the extent of squatting, but in realizing our worth in His eyes ...as even the common person with a stick—-called a shepherd in my dream—-could see.

(How can so many of us be so full of lack ...that we readily would defend a dunghill?? And at the same time, we often denounce the glorious majesty of our Lord, Jesus ...who came to save us.)

One more note: People often look at faith as a weakness, not a strength ...as if believing without evidence is weak and dumb. The Gospel of John, Chapter 20, verse 29 says, "Blessed are those who have not seen, and have believed."

It mentions those who have not seen because there are those who have. Noah's family saw (as did many others, but from a different perspective), the Israelites witnessed their miraculous escape from Pharaoh (as did the Egyptian troops), and many prophets of God were acknowledged by other nations. Many nations were astonished by victories and blessings bestowed upon God's people ...because they saw. Jesus performed miracles ...and many saw. The tomb of Jesus was empty ...though many tried to deny His resurrection. The Gospel of Matthew, Chapter 27, verses 52 & 53 speaks of many graves of people being opened after the resurrection of Jesus ...and they arose and went into the city where many people could see them.

So, many did see ...though it seemed to affect the people more when they saw and heard Jesus, and later the commitment of the apostles or disciples, and hearing what they were saying. What I'm saying is—-when we say, "You just need to have faith!"—-well, we are virtually saying one needs to believe something they have not seen, and they need to believe it by utilizing what they don't have ...which is faith.

So, to merely preach that they need to have faith ...it may fall on deaf ears. We may have to do what Isaiah 1:18 tells us ...the LORD says, "Come now, let us reason together."

(A bit of what I was trying to do with the first 5 Chapters.)

XVI.—-'Another King, but much we don't know ...'

God intended the relationship between husband and wife ...as designed by Him, to be one of the most cherished unions entered into when joined together with Him at the center.

Selah.

Post-selah ...

The King sends his servant to tell the woman to get off the streets ...if she wants to engage in that sort of activity, she needs to move beyond the outskirts of the city.

The servant returns with this word, "The woman said that in all due respect, she was not on the streets ...she said she was in her walled private courtyard, where no one would be able to see her. And she is married."

The King notices a slight smile, "Is there something amusing about all this?"

The servant quickly explains, "No, Your Excellency, I was just trying to remember what else she said."

The King asks rather abruptly, "Have you had adequate time to collect your thoughts? What else did she say?"

The servant hesitates, "I guess it was really nothing."

The King insists, "But, it is really something ...and I want to know what that something is."

The servant avoids eye contact, "Well, she just said that only someone from the castle wall could have seen her ...and no one within the King's noble employ would dare admit to the King that they gave a bathing woman more than a second glance."

The King commands, "Bring her to me ...so I can speak with her."

After much time, the woman enters the King's presence in her humble robes.

The King knows how intimidating this may seem, with her now standing before the King ...for uncertain reasons or consequences, "I apologize ...it was not my intent to violate your privacy, nor to assume fault on your part where none existed."

The woman's eyes meet his eyes, "I also apologize ...as I knew you'd be able to see me, and I don't know what came over me. Please forgive me."

The King steps closer. He doesn't mention that he knows she is married, wondering if she will pretend also.

The King peers into her soft eyes, "Excuse me for saying so, but you are a very beautiful woman ...anyone in my employ would gladly give you the attention that any woman deserves. And any one of my loyal soldiers would surely fight for the opportunity to have you as their wife."

The woman speaks softly, "That is the problem."

The King is a bit confused, "What is the problem?"

The woman begins to cry, "The fighting."

The King is trying to understand, "I didn't mean any of my soldiers would literally fight for you ...as if you were a prize of a brutal contest."

The woman attempts to wipe away the tears, "No, that's not what I meant ...not fighting for me. I am already married. It's just that with all the fighting, each soldier's wife could soon find herself without a husband. No one is challenging our borders ...why must we go outside the kingdom, looking for the next fight?"

The King attempts to defend his stance, "No one may be challenging us now, but if we appear weak to them ...well, that could all too quickly change."

The woman seeks his understanding, "I know that you truly loved the previous king's daughter ...and besides being common knowledge that he chased you all over the country, it's also no secret that during that time he gave your wife to another man. And though no one would dare say it in front of you, I dare say we all know that you and your armies killed many men ...and on occasion, when you killed a supposed enemy, you felt guilty when a couple women were left without their husbands, and no child. You also took those women as your wives ...so, was it perhaps out of your kindness, to make up for their loss? And how do you view the wives of your own soldiers? Do you also feel compassion for us? When our husbands die in battle, will you take all of us as your wives also?"

The King turns away for only a moment, then turns back to her, "If I make a habit of this, I will have no army to defend our kingdom ...but, I will make an exception for you. I will call for your husband ...and tell him he has served me well, but now he shall raise you a family, and you can both work for me here in the castle."

The woman's tears return, "I appreciate your concern, and what you are willing to do, but it will not work."

The King is assertive, "Of course it will work ...if the King commands something, it will be carried out."

The woman continues to cry, "That's not what I mean. I know my husband ...how loyal he is. He is so dedicated to the fight, if he is called back, he will still not sleep with me. He will beg to go back, and he is so committed to the fight ...he will eventually die, and will leave me with no child."

The King insists, "Please don't cry ...it is my weak point, seeing any woman cry. How could your husband possibly ignore you, if I called him back and told him to go to you? What can he imagine we all are fighting for? We fight so all women and children can hold within them the hope of having peace and safety. You are the reason we fight ...how can we ignore the very ones that we are fighting for?"

The woman continues to cry, "I don't know why he doesn't understand that ...but, he doesn't."

The King rests a comforting hand, and dries her tears with his robe, "Perhaps he would understand that giving you a child would be preserving our future army ...if it's a boy. And if it's a girl, perhaps she will be like you, and be able to help educate the rest of us less sensitive soldiers ...or kings."

XVII.—-'Song of Stephen'

I almost fell asleep, and my mind began to drift ...after beginning to read: The First Book of Kings & also Song of Solomon. And though I do not claim any interpretation, I am leaving you with my thoughts ...if you catch my drift.

(Also, we can say we have kindred spirits ...and better yet, is if we both have the knowledge to know about the Holy Spirit. Knowing about ...then to correctly follow His leading may seem to be an additional difficult step to many sincere people. Or it can be all too easy ...while easily, whether knowingly or not, bringing about a bit of spirit void of unity. How can that be?? That is another topic in itself ....entirely. But, I would like to say now ...thanks to those who've shared their insights through a book, entitled, '*Hard Sayings of the Bible*'. And yes, the section on "Song of Songs" was a pleasant and dreamy influence, while giving confidence to my drift. Thanks again!!)

Those who suffer, undoubtedly seek ...for peace, relief, or revenge.

While watching others suffer ...

????? What can be said of those who are compassionate? Do they seek to help console those who are suffering???

????? What of those who do nothing? In their mind, do they rationalize that they're not responsible for the suffering, and seek not to help? As a result of their lack of concern, if the suffering continues, do they eventually take notice, or do they remain cold and callous???

????? What of those who are opportunistic? Do they try to make sure the suffering continues ...as they blame someone other than themselves???

????? What of those who suffer along ...and often for long? May they reach out for answers difficult to find? Will they seek a depth of wisdom beyond themselves, searching for those answers???

Considering all *'strivings'*, those who only strive towards self-achievement ...may readily serve 'self' over others, and not serve God *'to the least of these'*.

One can acknowledge God, yet to what degree if not also acknowledging all those whom God loves. Understanding does not come immediately, but can be something we strive for.

Do not forfeit God's standard for us ...nor hold a standard we say is God's, without His compassion. We all make mistakes ...it's more significant how we move on afterwards.

Without God, the *'ecclesiastical'* conclusion can be said to be only vanity of vanities ...yes, all is vanity, without God.

Edited in a couple spots:

There have always been songs.

And songs are sung for particular occasions, for all sorts of particular reasons ...and they always express some feeling, whether it is lighthearted nonsense, or intensely emitted emotions.

Yes, songs are always sung, but the songs with the most meaning are those that need to be sung ...the most.

But sometimes the noted damage prevents it from being sung. Sometimes it is repressed by insane confusion or it is fearfully misunderstood, and can be uttered only through indiscernible agony.

There is a fine line between those considered civilized, and those who are not. There are, on occasion, exemplary individuals who live in a very uncivilized society ...and there are often very uncivilized people who live within a society that most people would hope to call civilized.

Sadly, it does seem to take a long time to convince a rather uncivilized group to become civilized, but a civilized group on occasion can become uncivilized rather quickly ...and I'm not talking about 'through a drunken condition'. I could be speaking of ideologies that often rapidly rise in our lives through those who attempt to incite and manipulate emotions ...birthed through discontentment, present prejudices, or perhaps hidden and often undetected deep-seated bitterness or anger.

No, that's not the end of the bad. Often there seems to be no limit. Sadly, there are those in life who embrace reprobate impulses ...beyond mere selfish aspirations, and void of any glimmer of regard for others.

The setting of this story is more than a thousand years ago, maybe more than two. There is not much of a standard of being civilized in most of the world, so it is quite common to be uncivilized. There is only one group of people that would hope to call themselves civilized, though they are being challenged within their own prideful claims to be so.

That which is uttered in the wood and in the field, might as well be uttered behind prison walls, as it is not heard. Many injustices and reprehensible acts echo throughout the valleys, but the sounds only return to self ...and the sounds are often as detested and shamed as the acts themselves.

Some observe the horrendous results of unacceptable passivity, tolerance, and a denial of all forms of guilt on anyone's part. When something that should be thoroughly confronted as unacceptable is ignored ...it becomes the part of ourselves that we often angrily deny is any part of our responsibility, or doing. Though aren't we really a part of that which we are not actively against? Just because we're not directly involved, does that somehow absolve us of our feelings of responsibility or guilt? Those questions do arise.

Yes, some detest the sounds, and try to wish them away. Some detest themselves because they are repeatedly taught to. The victims are taught they must not oppose the way of the world.

And some detest themselves, for only a moment, not knowing what to do ...and temporarily paralyzed, doing nothing. Perhaps a moment later, they still don't know what to do, but they decide they must do something.

Those in torment ...merely wait. They don't even know there are people who exist—-who'd bring relief, or a message of salvation.

And they don't have much hope. They begin with merely living each day ...to dreading each day. Or more accurately, dying each day ...or barely surviving each moment.

The majority of the people are oblivious to the comparative few who feel the agony inside. So, life goes on in the marketplace.

It's a busy place, and a most welcome change from the monotonous routine of everyday life. It also represents their livelihood ...and the ability to sell their goods, to have things they would otherwise not be able to have.

Binnie's parents think the people at the marketplace are no different than any other people; but her parents are just naive, sensing no hint of insincerity, and not to question the less than subtle staring glance.

Binnie does not like the marketplace. She is not one to want to draw attention to herself. Her clothes likely have been made from a burlap feed sack, yet they are looking beyond what she is wearing.

The fact is—-Binnie is only eight years old, but she cannot hide the beauty of her facial lines, nor the rapture of her lovely eyes—-and she looks nearly twice her age.

The people at the marketplace ask, "How old is your daughter? She's definitely growing up ...and in a little while, you'll probably let her come to the market by herself. You must be proud."

And she dreads when her dad says, "Yep, I guess in a year or so, we can stay home and just let Binnie take care of the *market run*."

Though Binnie feels uncomfortable with the marketplace, she doesn't quite know why. It's not that she's like any eight year old, with a desire to play, instead of doing work. She already does most of the work at home ...it's just that home is different.

Maybe she is making too much out of it. Maybe living in the country doesn't give you much of a chance to understand people ...or their ways.

But Binnie is content with not knowing much. And she is so relieved that 'market' is only once a year.

By the time the next year rolls around, she feels perhaps she'll look at the market differently, being a year older and more mature.

But the marketplace people don't look at her differently, they look at her more the same, and that intensifies when she hears dad say, "Yep, I think Binnie will be old enough to come to the market by herself next year."

At age nine, she feels she's capable of doing just about anything, but that doesn't mean she looks at everything as something she wants to do.

She would do almost anything for her parents, she loves them so much ...and it looks like that will include going to market by herself.

She keeps telling herself that it will be the same as it is now with her parents here ...they just won't be with her next time.

She can manage, she keeps telling herself.

But that next autumn comes too soon. As she arrives at the market, she soon realizes why she had hated it so much. The feeling of dread was not a fearful child's emotions, it was something she'd sensed ...now proved to be real.

Oh, how she wishes her parents were here. She absolutely doesn't know how to deal with this ...after all, she's just a child.

Binnie fears the time will never come ...but finally it is time to go home.

She wants to tell her parents, but as much as she wants to, and somehow imagines she will ...she doesn't.

She has enough money to give them. And she doesn't tell them she had barely sold any goods ...that she'd dumped the goods along the way, before she got home.

Each year, she'd tried to devise a new plan, to try to divert the dread ...but each time the marketplace seemed to be an even worse experience.

Finally, at age fifteen, when she arrives at the market, she sets up her stand ...but she resolves it will be her final stand.

She knew her parents had a particularly bad year and needed the money, but she was not going to do it again. All she has to do is survive this one last time ...and next year she will run away. Her parents will have to wonder what had happened to her. She loves them so much, but she cannot endure this much longer. Last year was the worst, and she can't imagine that this year will be any less dreadful ...it will probably be worse, if that is at all possible.

Binnie tries to separate herself from her emotions, as a group of men approach her.

They don't even seem the least bit subtle ...and they appear to be eyeing her up even more than the others.

What really concerns Binnie, is that when these men had approached, the other men had faded off into various other areas of the marketplace.

This new group of men circle about like a bunch of vultures, having scattered the regular men of prey ...successfully eliminating the competition.

What do this new group of men have in store for her?

With the old group, at least she could anticipate the end of the dread, as the market period closed. With these obviously greatly feared men dominating the scene, would she even be able to return home?

Binnie fears the most dreaded is about to come ...and feels she likely has seen home for the last time.

The one man who appears to be their leader, approaches her, "Where are your parents?"

Binnie doesn't know how to answer. She fears if she says they aren't here, then it will be all over for her ...perhaps their only hesitation is that they think her parents are here.

She doesn't answer.

She hears one of them whisper, "I wonder if she is a deaf-mute."

Another whispers, "No, I heard her talk briefly to someone when we first arrived."

The leader asks her, "How long are you to stay at the market?"

Binnie answers softly, "As long as I want ...and I'll be packing up soon."

She silently wishes they will be packing up soon, and leave her be.

The leader smiles, "I will buy up all your goods."

Binnie doesn't know what to think of this ...as the leader buys up all her goods. The wealth involved in such a huge transaction even scares her more. It seems there is no limit to what they are willing to do ...but why?

And she fears what reason may now come forth ...as she cannot understand why he pays her ten times the amount she was asking for.

The leader asks, "Do you have more?"

Binnie responds politely, "No, you've most generously bought all my goods."

The leader smiles and laughs, "Well, I guess you were right, you will be packing up soon."

Binnie is disturbed by his laugh, and he senses it, saying, "Don't be nervous, all I wish is to talk with your parents."

She is delighted to hear this, as she wants nothing more than to be safely at home with her parents again.

As the men follow Binnie on her long trip home, she thinks how relieved she is ...but she also resolves not to ever go to market again.

She has a plan.

When she gets home, she will give her parents the regular amount of money, but since the men had given her ten times as much, she will hide the rest of the money, and for the next nine years she will just pretend to go to market.

She will just dispose of the goods each year, and give them the amount of money she sets aside for that year.

Never in her life has she ever been so happy and relieved to see her parents.

But this feeling is short-lived, and is replaced by a feeling of betrayal. The men offer to pay her parents seventy times seven times the price they gave for the goods ...for her.

Binnie breaks down in tears as her parents eagerly accept the offer.

She has just been abandoned ...and the love she felt her parents had for her, actually only had a price.

She had thought her plan would help her escape the dread, but now it will have no effect ...she is literally doomed.

The leader realizes it even before he sees her tears. Being in the King's employ, one is used to taking orders without any thought of what effect it may have upon others. After all, the highest honor is serving the King.

But, the King had not ordered this ...they had taken it upon themselves. Everyone always scrambling to gain the favor of the King ...it should have dawned on him why the others had allowed him to lead with this one.

It was probably because they had doubts over their own suggestion ...but, so eager to lead, he now realizes he had failed as a leader. He should have known better, but he had eagerly told the King ...and now the King will be expecting him to deliver.

Having a daughter of his own, this leader feels he is, in a way, failing all daughters everywhere. With certain things it is difficult to hide the business of the King, and in this case they will likely know ...who is responsible.

The leader feels like running away ...and not returning to the King, but he knows he can't. His family will be eagerly waiting for him. His only course is that he must confess his failures to them, and try to salvage respect with the family's friends.

The leader is upset with himself for not thinking of it before. He should have taken his own daughter along.

The leader gives one of his men his own horse ...the fastest horse in the group, "Ride on ahead as fast as you can ride, and bring my daughter to meet us."

Several days go by ...and they travel on. Binnie is treated kindly, yet she still dreads for what purpose she was purchased ...and what awaits her.

Then the leader's daughter arrives. "My name is Tammy."

Binnie is not sure she can trust Tammy either, though she does have to admit she is a bit relieved.

She is guarded by what she asks, but she feels she must ask, "For what purpose was I purchased?"

Tammy does not hesitate to answer, "For the King."

Binnie cannot ask anymore. She begins to choke up with tears, and cannot speak.

Binnie cries throughout the night. Every time she perchance begins to fall asleep, she has a nightmare about the King, and she begins to cry again.

Tammy hears her crying, and silently crawls over to her side, whispering, "Binnie ...Binnie, I am so sorry! But let me tell you one thing ...I can help you escape!"

Binnie tries to break from her tears ...nodding in agreement that she will accept Tammy's help. And they both crawl off silently, gathering together some things and some food ...and off they go.

Perhaps a mile or so into the woods, Tammy says, "Let's stop here for a moment."

Binnie feels she can run for hours, "Why?"

Tammy insists, "There is something I must tell you."

Binnie listens, looking into Tammy's sincere eyes, dimly lit by the moonlight, "You have a choice, but I feel I must make clear the choices ...before you choose."

Binnie asks, "What do you mean, I thought we were running away?"

Tammy asks, "To what?"

Binnie pleas desperately, "To anything!"

Tammy begs to consider, "To those like at the marketplace? I know of those at the marketplace ...and I know of even worse."

Binnie cries, "Even worse, like ...maybe the King?"

Tammy is now crying, "No, the King is a very kind man ...he would kill anyone who would attempt to be unkind to you."

Binnie cries, "A kind man who would ...kill? I don't want to be near that kind of man!"

Tammy tries to help her understand, "No, he has many people guarding all the comings and goings at the palace ...no one would dare attempt anything, so he doesn't have to kill."

Binnie still continues to cry, "Why do they not dare attempt anything?"

Tammy simply states, "Because he's the King!"

Binnie nearly shouts, "Why did you take me out here to tell me this! I thought you were going to help me escape, now it sounds like you are trying to convince me to stay!"

Tammy wipes tears from her own eyes, "I wanted you to know I will support you with whatever choice you make. I helped you escape, and I will stand by that. But by letting you go, you will not be escaping. My dad conducted a legal transaction, and if you go home ...well, that's the first place he will go to look for you. If you simply run away and not go home, you will live in torment ...always wondering where you have to escape to next, and in constant danger of the kind of people you had to contend with at the marketplace. The only true escape is in going to the King."

Binnie is still in disbelief, "The true escape would've been ...in not viewing me as something that could be purchased, and letting me stay at home. I had a plan to avoid the marketplace. Now, I'm the one who was sold. I may be some precious commodity to some sick man, but being sold and subjected to the whims of others is of no precious value to me ...and it is not freedom. The King undoubtedly has unknown riches, and can buy most anything he wants, but I ask you how you can consider him kind ...with no consideration of how I feel. Do you know what I call that? I say the King is a sick man."

Tammy's eyes gather in all the moonlight, "How did you know the King was sick?"

The next thing Binnie knows, she is standing before the King.

The King says, "You are very beautiful. I tell you the truth that I have not seen anyone in my entire kingdom, nor in my live-long days ...as beautiful as you."

Binnie tries to be strong, but cannot hold back the tears. She is not fooled by those words. Those words are the same whispers of the marketplace ...and she is well aware of the dread that follows.

She gushes forth in tears, standing before the King's bed ...with the King in bed, as she anticipates what is expected of her.

The King calls forth, "Tammy, would you come in here, please?"

Tammy also stands before the King.

The King speaks to Binnie, "I am old ...and I am very ill. You have been purchased as a gift for me. I knew little of what it would entail. I have already talked with Tammy, and from what she has said ...and from the things she said you did not say, I can imagine. I know the marketplace, and what vile creatures roam there. I am so sorry what you've had to endure. I would like you to stay a couple days, to rest from your long journey. Then I will have my men bring you back home. Your parents can keep all the money given for your purchase ...as I consider it an invaluable lesson to me. I will send two soldiers to stay with the three of you ...to guarantee safety to you and your parents."

Binnie manages two words, through her tears, "Thank you!"

The King smiles, "You must be tired of the same food every day from your long journey. Tammy, you can take Binnie to the berry patch by the lake. She should enjoy that."

Two days later, Binnie is assisted by the two soldiers, for the long journey home.

She is so eager to get home, though she feels kind of awkward too. For the first time in her life, she has to deal with the doubts of their love for her ...having so readily agreed to her purchase.

Upon arriving home, she finds another family living there.

It is clear her parents had sold the farm ...having no tie to her, or to the home she had cherished for all these years.

The two soldiers assist Binnie in inquiring of her parents' whereabouts, but no one knows ...aside from the fact that they'd purchased many things that would enable them to travel ...to where, no one knows.

The two soldiers tell Binnie that they must report back to the King; that they'd been unable to accomplish their task. As kindly as they can, they explain to her that they were employed to guard her ...and must continue to do so.

Binnie says she understands, and agrees to travel back with them.

After the long journey back, they finally arrive back at the palace.

Binnie asks the two soldiers if she can first go to the berry patch by the lake.

She quickly picks all the huge juicy berries she can find. She doesn't eat any herself. She smiles, "Now, let's go to the King!"

Binnie brings the King the fully ripe berries, and the soldiers explain what had happened.

After the soldiers finish explaining, Binnie takes a deep breath before boldly addressing the King, "I'd like to stay to serve you, if you will have me!"

Binnie spends the next several years serving the King cold fresh water, a variety of fresh fruits and berries, and she has the craftsmen build huge wooden wheels for the King's bed ...so she can wheel him throughout the castle, and even out into the fragrant gardens and orchard.

The King has the joy of a child, and Binnie takes on the role of the parent, or the caretaker ...and both are totally content with taking on those roles.

Those years are the best years Binnie has ever experienced, but it comes to an end.

The King ...dies.

Confusion abounds throughout the kingdom.

Binnie is scared. The palace is about with whispers, and the constant chatter of those seeking advantage. The King had many sons, and it is uncertain who will reign next. And one of the sons begins to look at her in much the same way as those at the marketplace had.

Turmoil heightens until the son who'd been looking at her ...appears to be the next to reign.

Then suddenly it appears that another son will be the one to reign. The one who makes her feel uncomfortable by the way he looks at her, loses his support and has to accept the fact that he will not become King as he thought he would. But as sort of a consolation, he does ask for one thing ...for Binnie to be his wife.

Binnie is very scared by this ...thinking he may rule his household much like the marketplace was run. But then she doesn't see him anymore. After hearing his request to obtain her as his wife, he is no longer seen about, nor does anyone mention what happened to him.

Though Binnie can't help being curious about what happened to him, she is even more relieved.

And Binnie is told she forever has a place in the King's palace.

This new King restores the kingdom back to the way it was during his dad's reign ...there is no turmoil, and everyone is in agreement and at peace.

The King seems to enjoy lavishing upon many women. Binnie spends most of her time with Tammy, and tries to stay out of everyone else's way. But she can't help notice the King's way.

The King seems to really enjoy entertaining other kingdoms ...and the King is gifted with many riches of these kingdoms, as well as the promised delights of their daughters.

Binnie cannot forget her past. She remembers all too well the time she was purchased, yet what she recalls most is the love she felt in being set free from this confusing genre of rituals and courtship ...not being subjected to what these women so freely seem eager to employ in. While at first feeling she'd been purchased as a mere commodity, she later felt that, in truth, her freedom had been purchased. While these other women seem all too eager to enjoy the commodity of presenting themselves, and trying to put forth their fine qualities as admirable selling points.

* * * * * * * *

At this time, I must take a slight aside with the story ...the story I call, the *'Song of Stephen'*. Having worked in a prison, I know how confining that must seem. I also know that there are cultures throughout the world who accept the existence of a home being even more 'confining' than a prison ...or a place one is asked to call home. But having worked in a prison, I've also witnessed how effective a television can be in occupying time. Knowing enough about the content of television, it certainly is my belief that today's viewing of television has little potential value towards possible rehabilitation of prisoners ...and little teaching value, in general, for our children whom we hope will avoid the prison system. Yet, it is not just prison that we should fear. There is much danger in allowing ourselves to be absorbed in some things that are not illegal. A co-worker of mine, by the name of Charles, gave me his assessment one evening. There was a sporting event on television that he would have preferred to see, but the prisoners and a couple of the female co-workers wanted to see the television show entitled, *'The Bachelor'*. I had not seen the show, nor had any desire to ...and what he described brought me no closer to any inclination to. Reportedly, there was a millionaire or multi-millionaire, so-called gentleman, who 'made show' of entertaining the thought of a wife being chosen out of a dozen women applicants. Each week he'd hand out roses to those still in contention. Yet, I don't know why I'm telling you this—-because most of you know more about the show than I do—-and I still contend that I never want to watch it.

But my point of why I am telling you this, is that, in my story, Binnie didn't want to see the show either. Yet, unlike the show on television ...where each week women were eliminated, the show with the King added new women each week, it seemed. And the King would lavish the new woman with compliments, and present her with gifts. And the next week, another woman would be the recipient of the same compliments, and be showered with equal gifts.

* * * * * * * *

Binnie did not understand why each woman appeared to be delighted to have her turn, but that seemed to be the way it was.

And Binnie did not look forward to the day when perchance the King would approach her, and it would be her turn. It seemed to her that all these kindnesses were an actual show put on, not just feeding the King's desires, but slowly allowing her to see his kindness ...and perhaps learn to be like everyone else, in accepting it.

Binnie thought the day may come, but then tried to convince herself that things were not as they seemed.

But the day did come, and she was as frightened as she'd been that first day when she'd stood before this King's dad ...when he had been King.

Binnie does not see this as a gradual process of learning of the King's kindness. Yes, he was kinder and more a gentleman than most ...and much different than the King's brother had been, whom she had never again seen. But all this kindness and gentlemanliness did not come close to love, the love she had felt from this King's dad, who had seemed to understand that the greatest love he could show was in setting her free.

And she had shown her greatest love in return, by voluntarily returning to freely serve him.

The King speaks softly, "You are the most beautiful and most precious of all women in my kingdom, and of kingdoms afar."

He begins to compliment Binnie as he had the others ...and shower her with gifts. But the King sees her hesitation in accepting the gifts ...and he sees her tears.

Anyone would want the opportunity to hold and console such a beautiful woman, but the King sees more than that. The King sees that others who had likely attempted to rob her of her innocence ...had hurt her greatly in doing so.

He also realizes that the others who had hurt her, though not as mannerly or as gentlemanly as he ...may appear in her eyes, as all the same. To her, he was being as much like them, as he was not like them. And the truth of that brings the King to an uncomfortable realization.

He, too, was looking at her not as a person, and not for what he could give her, but rather for what she could give him.

It was at this moment that he realized that true love could only be given to her as his dad had given her. His dad had given Binnie her innocence back. He had truly loved her ...and she had truly loved him for that.

The King suddenly realizes that all that he had been seeking, after all, was not love. And now that he'd found what true love was, he could only have it by not having her.

Yes, it is now clear to the King. Binnie had loved his dad in a way that he, as the son, had previously not understood. And by not respecting that love, which she still clings onto so dearly in her heart, he would be robbing her of the only love she ever knew. No one could replace, nor could add to that love. There is no enhancing that which exists in its purest form.

The King speaks softly to Binnie, "You will no longer reside in my palace."

Binnie hopes the King has not misinterpreted her feelings. She does not want to be sent away; she has appreciated the safety and security ...and everything that has been provided for her. Yet, she realizes the King has every right to send her away.

Binnie wonders what it will be like.

She had become quite accustomed to living without fear, and virtually not having anything to worry about. Will those of the marketplace be waiting for her? Has she been too selfish, clinging to what she had with the King's dad?

Perhaps she should accept the King as the other women have, and not think of the love in her heart. She would not be happy, but a little dread is arguably better than the marketplace.

But deep inside she knows it won't work. How can she serve the King ...and pretend she is like those other women, when she is not.

She had loved this King's dad as a daughter should love her father—-and the King's dad had loved her as a father loves his daughter. If only this King would realize the love his dad had for her, and as a memorial of that love, if only he would show love in much the same way ...then she wouldn't be having this dilemma.

She cannot merely hope to savor within her a love as it should be, which she once had, then suddenly turn from it, trusting the roads of the world to better lead her ...making a mockery of love, at the very place she first realized it.

But before she can say anything, the King calls for his two main soldiers ...and Binnie prepares to be forever banished. The King had already declared that she would no longer reside in his palace.

"Guards ...escort Binnie out of my palace! Take her to the place I spoke to you earlier about. As you know, Binnie, my dad is buried by the cottage at the lake, upon his request. He died before he could make any request for you, but I think I know what it would have been. You will live out the rest of your days, and I pray they will be years aplenty ...tending to the berry patches, the fragrant orchards, and the gardens surrounding my dad's gravesite. I believe it is there you will be most happy ...and it is there I believe my dad would have liked you to be."

Binnie cannot speak through her tears, but her eyes speak of appreciation ...and she forms the words, thank you, silently with her mouth.

At that very moment, the King realizes that this is the greatest gift he has ever given ...and the greatest he has ever received.

The King shouts away his own tears, "And gather the musicians together, for tonight they will play ...for today, I've realized the true song of my own heart. It is a song which is not my own, but it is one of harmony ...one of joy ...eternal joy."

XVIII.—-'Our daughter's story ...'

'All About Zebras' ...written and illustrated by Leah

> *Dedicated to: Jesus ...He made zebras*
> *Hello!*
> *Zebras are my favorite animals. My name is Leah. I am 4 years old.*
> *I have a stuffed zebra named 'Zebra-boy'. He goes with me places. Mom will help me write a story about zebras.*
> *Once there was a zebra named 'Stripe'. He had a very nice family.*
> *"I love my family", said Stripe. "We are very close and stick together."*
> *"Sometimes we don't get along, but we know we can forgive each other and be kind again. We know we are safer when we stick together."*
> *"There are some guys that try to catch us. We can run very fast."*
> *When Jesus comes back the lion will lay down with the lamb ...and zebras too!!!*
> *"Sometimes people come and take us to the zoo. The zebras do get food, water, and lots of attention, but being free is best of all. What do you think?!?*
> *It took a long time to write my zebra book. It was fun.*
> *My Dad is writing a book too.*
> *Tomorrow is my birthday. I will be five.*
> *The last page has zebra facts, family & friends.*
> *Bye!*

(Of course, that was over two decades ago ...yet, it has taken me quite some time to get published also.)

XIX.—-'Head Hydro, Supreme Sul, & the Big Ox'

Suppose things were different than they are now (not intended to be a Twilight Zone beginning).

Intelligence was somewhat consuming ...and all substances were flammable gases, and the active burning was the fuel for their intelligence. (not intended to be like Star Trek either)

Most everything was either (not ether) hydrogen, second in abundance was oxygen, and there was slightly less sulfur. (let's move on ...and not to boldly go where no one has gone before)

With the intelligence, there was defined leadership ...whether self-appointed, or just generally and mutually accepted. There was the head Hydro, the big Ox, and the supreme Sul ...as they were called. The supreme sulfur was named Lou ...or more commonly called Lou Sulfur.

Lou was the brightest of the Sulfur group, and with increased intelligence there was an increased realization of a personal force that the others did not know about. They all had this force, but they just didn't realize it.

When Lou told the rest of the Sulfur group about it, they began to gravitate towards him.

So absorbed in himself ...Lou was certain he could soon convince all the others to be also (absorbed, that is). As they gravitated towards Lou, he got larger and larger, and none that got near him could resist him ...they all became a part of him.

Soon both the Hydrogen and Oxygen groups saw what was happening, but though they individually outnumbered him, they felt powerless to do anything about it ...fearing they'd soon all be consumed, one by one.

There was only one thing they could do ...and that was to give up their own individuality, to combine themselves together.

But they couldn't do it the way Lou Sulfur was doing it, they'd all be consumed together. Though nearly a third of the others had done it, it was out of the question for this remaining group to combine with Lou Sulfur, as that would be playing right into his hands.

There were many more Hydrogens, so each Oxygen decided to join forces with two Hydrogens. They knew it would be the end for them ...at least for who they once were, but it was the only way.

Truthfully, it wasn't the only way ...as Sul was only pseudo supreme. As it was, the truly Supreme only wanted to see if the others would sacrifice their very existence for the higher purpose.

The Sul group had literally done that also, but it was a matter of seeking ConSul, being 'conned' into believing that which was not higher ...sacrificing for their own unforeseen inevitable loss.

The Hydrogen and Oxygen groups combined to become a water molecule, understanding there likely would be no turning back.

And with a flood of emotions, I mean, water, they extinguished Lou Sulfur ...ending his fiery existence. Or at least they thought so ...as who knew then, what the future would hold?

Well, you may find this story interesting, and even somewhat entertaining ...but, of course, you all knew that I made it up. Not being my favorite subject, I believe this is my first story about gas ...and yes, maybe I could have solidified more of what I was attempting to say. I admit that it was a bit watered down. And I will add a note, in lieu (Lou) of what's been said.

* ****** *

(A note here: We have five children ...and we love them so much. We had occasion to watch *'Star Wars'* together. I was surprised that they presented a case for defending Darth Vader. They said that he was unable to kill his son when it came down to that ...and he instead turned on the one who had driven him to the 'dark side'. And they presented that case even before they saw the 'back story', or the prequels, as they call them—-which often help us understand what led up to what the person had become, through a series of events in the person's life. Yet, there are those like the character 'Palpatine' who acts the role of a nice guy—-though when we see what he is actually about—-he shows no signs of changing, passes up every opportunity to change, and actually appears to get worse. I tried to address this concept with another character (not in *'Star Wars'*) in *'The Essence ...'*, part 1 of *'The Evolution of Confusion'* ...where one of the characters had been given so much, and still continued down that path of opposition and ingratitude. It does happen sometimes that way. But, for those who do seem to change ...there are those like our children who reach out and forgive. I think that is partly because they know they are loved by Dad & Mom ...but, more so because they know the love of God. Watching all those Jesus movies together has certainly impacted that message ...and who can resist the loving character of Jesus?)

XX.—-'The End'

As 4-year-old Leah once said, "Bye!"

(Of course, with me ...saying, "the end" is sort of a fanciful or wishful idea. But let's be real—-have you ever got off that easy with me?)

Beside this book, there are a baker's dozen more:
We Should Also Love One Another
Who Would Not Want an Inheritance?
What is His Name?
Am I Trying to Take Away From Jesus?
Questions of the Heart
(And a series of eight):
So Loved .../The Curious Whether and How/Do the Birds in the Wilderness, Not Heard, Stop Singing Their Songs?/The Evolution of Confusion—-1 thru 5

(Some people have the gift of encouragement and edification ...and I'm not asking anyone to be blunt or crass, but perhaps there are times the truth should be known. My poem on the following pages bears that out. Something else that bears mentioning is that I've never been accused of writing anything that has been considered a 'page-turner', so you don't have to struggle with your gift of encouragement around me—-I'm used to hearing crickets. And I like crickets. Yet again, let me now be 'the encourager'—-there are only six pages left to read, so *you can do it!!* And who knows, perhaps I've saved the best for last. If not ...it *is* 'the end'.)

'Afterthoughts/Epilogue/Final thoughts'

The best storytellers that I know are writers or speakers who bring relevance to everyday life, giving it actual meaning ...whether communicated through books, movies, friends & family, or Pastor Tom (and Myron, the Associate Pastor, both dear friends).

Writers who tell the best stories, in my opinion, bring meaning to the lives of their characters. And sometimes those characters are us. So, that's why I feel that every week I get the *best* ...whether it be the Pastor, or the Associate Pastor. And I attend a rather small church, so I don't feel like a *'nobody'.*

I also enjoy the messages from Rick and Aalden, and the many other friendships and kind words exchanged between so many friends. Yet one of my greatest joys throughout the years has been my children's laughter ...and Grandpa was always best at making them laugh.

Sometimes it is not the stories, or the messages ...but there is great meaning in the relationship with the person. I absolutely love being around family. And I love that God truly relates and brings great meaning to our life ...wanting us to understand. And personally, the relationship with Jesus makes it all meaningful. Understanding God allows me to enjoy life and gives me a different focus—-so I can be more understanding of others who may be struggling—-and I can convey to them a bit more love, showing them that love does have meaning.

The third King of Israel, Solomon, wrote: *"A time to break down, and a time to build up; a time to weep, and a time to laugh."* With me, perhaps there's a time to scratch your head. I know I can use a bit of action up there. Stimulating a little growth can be a good thing. But if you are *breaking down*, I'd say a few tears are a natural and healthy outlet ...yet, we need to allow God to build us back up.

There are times I am very serious, but I also find many occasions for healthy and appropriate laughter.

I'm thankful God provides me both. And I wish the same for you.

(Yes, end with a 'page-turner' ...be bold, turn the page.)

'Sorry, not finished ...a closing poem'

It so happens there was this couple,
   whose last name was actually, 'Love'.
   And though marriage is what they experienced,
   later it's what they were the most afraid of.

It all started with a disagreement,
   that some would call a fight.
   But it was just a difference of opinion,
   there was no show of might.

They were about to have a baby,
   and experience all the joy that brings.
   But they had a disagreement over the name of the child,
   of all the silly things.

She said, "Our child should be Clotilda or Bartram,
   named after my mom or dad."
   He said, "No way, perhaps Chloe or Bart,
   those other names aren't very rad."

Well, that really hurt her feelings,
   his tone of voice wasn't right.
   And the fact that *love* wasn't there,
   was the only agreement that night.

But Love came the next morning,
    in the form of a little girl.
    Except *their* love hadn't reconciled,
    and it was about to unfurl.

At that very moment, it was agreed
    their child should never experience this.
    So both of them firmly decided
    their daughter would always remain a 'Miss'.

Now how to accomplish this,
    with love all around,
    may not be so easy as it seems.
    They would have to come up with a plan,
    a surefire one,
    that would thwart any notions or dreams.

They'd have to make quite certain
    that love would never get a start.
    They'd have to thwart the beginnings,
    and turn away every pining heart.

And that's where they got back to the discussion,
    about that precious name.
    It would have to be one that'd give no spark,
    no chance to fan the flame.

It's hard to believe they'd do this;
    why does anyone do what one does?
    But this Miss Love, she'd *miss love*;
    that's just the way it was.

As she got older, there were many friendly boys
    who were certainly up to the task.
    Showing their mannerly ways, she was the first one
    they'd usually approach and ask.

"What's your name?" She'd then reply, "I'm Taken,"
    and they'd quickly all turn away.
    She couldn't quite figure it out, "Why am I so forsaken?"
    she'd often cry and pray.

Then one day a man strolled up,
    and smiled at her with eyes of blue.
    "You must be Miss Taken,
    but I'm afraid we've all been mistaken too."

Soon they were both laughing,
    the first time she'd laughed in years.
    A few years later, they married;
    she said, "I do!" with happy tears.

The thing we can learn from this,
    is that love can disagree.
    Realizing this, can make the difference,
    and it can set us free.

Now love is not always what it seems,
    and it's not truly everywhere.
    But you can always find it,
    it's the one thing more I'd like to share.

Love is not merely *something* we pray *for*,
    it's the *One* we need to pray *to*.
    Love is God, and God is love ...
    He is love, through and through.

But God is also 'righteousness',
    so please don't disagree.
    He sent His Son, to show us,
    as He died on Calvary.

And if we don't follow love,
    the way God shows us as true.
    We will just sadly find ourselves,
    among the *mistaken* too.